COLLECTION

by Lauren Tarshis

illustrated by Scott Dawson

Scholastic Inc.

TABLE OF CONTENTS

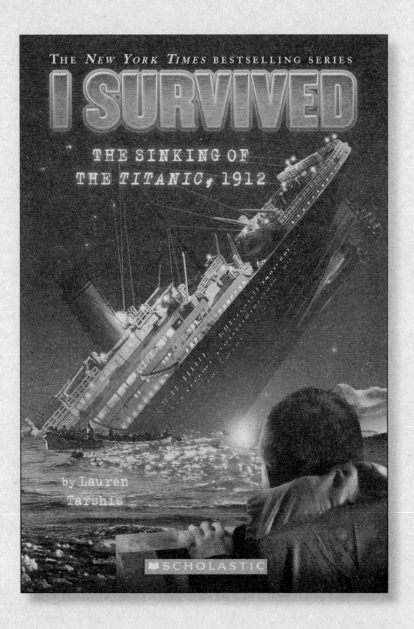

I SURVIVED

THE SINKING OF
THE *TITANIC*, 1912

by Lauren Tarshis

illustrated by Scott Dawson

Scholastic Inc.

CHAPTER 1

The *Titanic* was sinking.

The gigantic ship had hit an iceberg.

Land was far, far away.

Ten-year-old George Calder stood on the deck.

He shivered because the night was freezing cold.

And because he was scared. More scared than he'd ever been before.

More scared than when Papa swore he'd send George to the army school, far from everything and everyone.

More scared, even, than the time the black panther chased him through the woods back home in Millerstown, New York.

The deck of the *Titanic* was packed with people. Some were running and shouting.

"Help us!"

"Take my baby!"

"Jump!"

Some just plain screamed. Children cried. A gunshot exploded across the deck. But George didn't move.

Just hold on, he told himself, gripping the rail. Like maybe he could hold up the ship.

He couldn't look down at that black water. He kept his eyes on the sky. He had never seen so many stars. Papa said that Mama watched over him from heaven.

Could Mama see him now?

The ship lurched.

"We're going down!" a man shouted.

George closed his eyes, praying this was all a dream.

Even more terrible sounds filled the air. Glass shattering. Furniture crashing. More screams and cries. A bellowing sound, like a giant beast was dying a terrible death. George tried to hold the rail. But he lost his grip. He tumbled, smashing his head on the deck.

And then George couldn't see anything.

Even the stars above him seemed to go black.

CHAPTER 2

George woke up early that morning, half expecting to hear Papa calling him for chores.

But then he remembered: the *Titanic*!

He was on the greatest ship in the world.

It was their fifth day at sea. George and his

eight-year-old sister, Phoebe, had spent two months in England with their aunt Daisy. What a time they had! As a surprise for George's tenth birthday, Aunt Daisy took them to see the Tower of London, where they used to chop off your head if the king didn't like you.

Now they were heading back to America.

Back to Papa and their little farm in upstate New York.

George got out of bed and knelt by the small, round window that looked out on the ocean.

"Morning," said Phoebe, peering through the silk curtains of her bed and fumbling for her spectacles. Her curly brown hair was practically standing straight up. "What were you looking for?"

George had to smile. Phoebe always had a question, even at the crack of dawn.

Maybe that's why she was the smartest little sister in the world.

"I thought I saw a giant squid," George said. "And it's coming to get us!"

George rushed over and grabbed Phoebe with wiggly squid arms. She curled up into a ball and laughed.

She was still laughing when Aunt Daisy came in. Even in her robe and slippers, Aunt Daisy was the prettiest lady on the whole ship. Sometimes George couldn't believe she was so old: twenty-two!

"What's this?" Aunt Daisy said. "You know the rule: No having fun without me!"

Phoebe sat up and put her arms around George. "Georgie said he saw a giant squid."

Aunt Daisy laughed. "I wouldn't doubt it. Everyone wants to get a look at the *Titanic*. Even sea monsters."

George halfway believed it. He'd never imagined anything like the *Titanic*.

Aunt Daisy called the ship a floating palace. But it was way better than the cold and dusty castles they'd seen in England. They had three whole rooms—one for Phoebe and George, one for Aunt Daisy, and one for sitting around and doing nothing. They even had a man, a steward named Henry. He had bright red hair and an Irish accent that made everything he said sound like a jolly song.

"Some fresh towels for your bath?" he would say. "Some cocoa before bed?"

And just before they turned out the lights for the night, Henry would knock on their door and peep his head in.

"Is there anything else you might need?" he'd ask.

George kept trying to think of *something* he needed.

But what could you ever need on the *Titanic*?

The ship had everything, even a swimming pool with ocean water heated up like a bath, even gold silk curtains for your bed so you could pretend you were sleeping in a pirate's den, even three dining rooms where you could eat anything you wanted. Last night George had eaten two plates of roast beef, veal and ham pie, carrots sweet as candy, and a mysterious dessert called meringue pudding. It tasted like sugary clouds.

Actually, there *was* one thing missing from the *Titanic*: the New York Giants baseball team. George wondered what Henry would say if George said, "I need shortstop Artie Fletcher right away!"

Probably Henry would say, "Coming right up, sir!"

George grinned just thinking about it.

But Aunt Daisy wasn't smiling at him. She looked very serious.

"We have to make the most of our last three days at sea," Aunt Daisy said in a low voice. "I want you to promise me, George. *No more* trouble!"

George gulped.

Was she really still mad at him for last night?

He'd slid down the banister of the grand staircase in the first class lobby. How could he

resist? The wood was so shiny and polished, curving around like a ride at the fair.

"That lady could have moved out of the way," George said.

"How could she?" Phoebe said. "She was wearing a hundred pounds of diamonds!"

Aunt Daisy almost smiled. George could tell.

No, she could never stay mad at George for long.

Aunt Daisy put her face very close to George's. She had freckles on her nose, just like George and Phoebe.

"No more trouble," she repeated, tapping his chest. "I don't want to have to send a telegram to your father."

George's stomach tightened into a baseball.

"Don't tell Papa!" Phoebe said. "He'll send George away to that army school!"

"I'll be good," George promised. "I will, really."

"You better be," Aunt Daisy said.

CHAPTER 3

George didn't mean to get into trouble.

It's just that he got these *great* ideas.

Like on their first day at sea, when he had climbed up the huge ladder into the crow's nest.

"Aunt Daisy!" he'd yelled, waving his arms.

She had looked up. And she'd almost fainted.

And yesterday George had explored the entire ship. Aunt Daisy kept warning him that he'd get lost. She said the ship was like a maze. But George could always find his way. Even in the huge forest that stretched out behind their farm. Mama used to say that George had a map of the world behind his eyes.

He saw the engine rooms and the boiler rooms, and wound up on the third-class recreation deck. He was watching some boys play marbles when he noticed that he wasn't alone. A little boy was staring up at him with huge eyes the color of amber glass.

"See," the boy said. "See."

And he held out a postcard of the Statue of Liberty. He looked so proud, like he'd carved that big lady himself. George felt like he had to show something in return, so he took out his good-luck charm, the bowie knife Papa had given him for his ninth birthday. He let the little boy run his fingers across the handle, which was carved from an elk's antler.

"Enzo," the little boy said, puffing out his chest and pointing to himself.

"George," said George.

"Giorgio!" the little boy cried with a smile.

A man sitting near them laughed. He was reading an Italian-English dictionary and had the same huge eyes as the boy. George guessed right that he was Enzo's father.

"Marco," he said, shaking George's hand. "You are our first American friend."

Marco must have been studying that dictionary pretty hard, because George understood everything he said. George learned that Enzo was four years old. He'd lost his mama too. He and Marco came from a little town in Italy, and now they were moving to New York City. George told Marco about their farm and their trip and explained that any decent person living in New York had to be a Giants fan. For some reason, Marco thought that was funny.

When it was time for George to leave, Enzo got upset. Very upset.

"Giorgio!" he howled, loud enough for the entire ship to hear.

People stared and put their hands over their ears. Marco promised that they'd see George again, but Enzo wouldn't quit howling. George had never heard anything so loud.

By the time Enzo let go of George's leg and George ran back up to the suite, Aunt Daisy was practically howling too.

"I thought you fell overboard!" she cried.

But even then she wasn't really mad.

She didn't get *really* mad until last night.

How that lady screamed when George came sliding down the banister — like he really was a giant squid.

George didn't mind getting yelled at. He was used to it. Not a day at school went by without Mr. Landers shouting "George! Settle down!" And Papa, well, he always seemed to be mad at George.

But not Aunt Daisy. And being on this trip was supposed to make her happy, happy for the first time since her husband died last year. It had been Uncle Cliff's dream to be on the maiden voyage of the *Titanic*. He'd struck it rich selling automobiles and had plenty of money to pay for one of the biggest suites on the ship.

When Uncle Cliff had his accident, George was sure Aunt Daisy would cancel the trip. Instead she'd invited George and Phoebe to go with her.

And to George's shock, Papa said they could.

"Your aunt's going on this trip to find a little peace," he'd said to George. "I expect you to be a perfect gentleman."

And if he wasn't, George knew he'd be shipped off to that army school for sure. Papa had been talking about that place ever since George had brought the two-foot rat snake to school to show Mr. Landers—because they were studying reptiles!

George had been perfect the whole time in England. He'd let Aunt Daisy drag him to a fancy clothes store for a new pair of boots. He even learned to drink tea without spitting it back into the cup.

But, well, the *Titanic*.

The ship gave him so many great ideas!

But now he'd really be perfect.

No more ideas for the rest of the voyage.

CHAPTER 4

Phoebe wasn't taking any chances with George.

"I'm not letting you out of my sight," she announced after they'd finished breakfast. "I'm your guardian angel."

"I didn't know angels wore spectacles," he said, tugging on one of Phoebe's curls.

"The smart ones do," Phoebe said, grabbing George's arm. She offered him a lemon drop from the little silver tin she'd been carrying around since London.

George made a face. He hated those old-lady candies.

George wanted to go find Marco and Enzo and hear more about Italy. He wanted to ride the elevators up and down. Hardly any other ship in the world had elevators! Better yet, he wanted to find Mr. Andrews, the ship's designer.

When Mr. Andrews had stopped by their table at dinner the first night, George thought he was just another boring millionaire coming over to kiss Aunt Daisy's hand.

But Mr. Andrews was different.

"You *built* the *Titanic*?" said George.

Mr. Andrews smiled. "Not by myself. It took thousands of men to build her. But I did design her, that's true."

He invited George and Phoebe to come with him to the first class writing room. He unrolled the ship's blueprints across a long, polished table.

It was like looking at the skeleton of a giant beast.

"She's the biggest moving object ever built," Mr. Andrews explained. "Eleven stories tall. Forty-five thousand tons of steel. And longer than four city blocks."

"Our aunt says nothing bad can happen to this ship," Phoebe said. "People say it's unsinkable."

"No ship is safer," Mr. Andrews said. "That is certainly true."

"What if the *Titanic* was hit by a meteor?" said Phoebe, whose latest obsession was outer space. She was determined to see a shooting star before they docked in New York.

Mr. Andrews didn't laugh or roll his eyes like Mr. Landers did when Phoebe asked her questions.

"I hadn't planned on any meteors hitting the ship," Mr. Andrews said thoughtfully. "But I'd like to think she could take almost anything and still float."

Phoebe seemed satisfied.

"Are there any secret passages?" said George.

Mr. Andrews studied his blueprints, and then pointed to the boiler rooms.

"There are escape ladders," he said. "They run up the starboard side of the ship, up two decks, through the stokers' quarters, and into their dining hall. I hear the crew likes using them instead of the stairs."

George could have stayed there all night. He

asked a million questions and Mr. Andrews answered every single one.

"I was like you when I was a boy," Mr. Andrews said just before Aunt Daisy came to haul George off to bed. "One day I predict you'll build a ship of your own."

George knew that would never happen. He could barely get through a day at school. But he liked that Mr. Andrews said it. And he sure wanted to find those secret ladders.

But Phoebe had different ideas.

First she dragged George to the first class library so she could check out a book on Halley's comet. Then she took him on a walk on the boat deck. He felt like a dog.

"Strange," Phoebe said, looking at the life-boats that hung just off the deck. "There are only sixteen boats. That's not nearly enough for everyone."

"The ship's unsinkable," George said. "So do we really need lifeboats at all?"

Phoebe stared at the boats and shrugged. "I guess you're right," she said. And then she announced that it was time to see how many ladies were wearing hats with blue feathers.

George groaned.

This would be the most boring day of his life.

But at least nobody was yelling at him.

CHAPTER 5

At dinner that night, Aunt Daisy raised her glass. "To George! No trouble for one entire day!"

They clinked their glasses together just as an old man stopped by their table.

"Mrs. Key," the man said to Aunt Daisy. "I've been meaning to say hello."

"Mr. Stead!" Aunt Daisy said. "What a pleasure. This is George, my nephew, and Phoebe, my niece."

Mr. Stead nodded hello.

"So," Aunt Daisy said. "What brings you onto this magnificent ship?"

"Oh, I couldn't miss it," he said. "I think all of society is on this ship. I hear there's even an Egyptian princess on board."

"Really!" Aunt Daisy said. "I haven't met her!"

"Well, none of us have. She's traveling in the first class baggage room."

"Excuse me?" Aunt Daisy said.

"The princess is more than twenty-five hundred years old," Mr. Stead said.

George's ears perked up.

"I'm not sure I understand," Aunt Daisy said.

"She's a mummy," Mr. Stead said.

"A mummy!" Phoebe gasped.

"That's right," Mr. Stead said. "From a tomb near Thebes. I understand she belongs to a man named Mr. Burrows. People are saying he sold the coffin to the British Museum. Then he packed the princess herself in a wooden crate. Apparently he's bringing her back for his collection. Some say it's bad luck to take a mummy from its tomb."

"I'm glad I'm not the superstitious type!" Aunt Daisy said.

Mr. Stead chuckled. "In any case, nothing can harm this ship. Not even the curse of a mummy!"

Mr. Stead tipped his hat and said good-bye.

"Mr. Stead is a very famous writer in England," Aunt Daisy said. "You never know who you'll meet on the *Titanic*!"

And then it hit George, the best idea ever.

That mummy! He had to see it.

Maybe this day wasn't so boring after all.

CHAPTER 6

George didn't tell Phoebe or Aunt Daisy about his plan.

He figured he'd head down to the first class baggage room after they went to sleep. He'd find Mr. Burrows's crate, pry it open, and take a quick peek at the mummy. He'd be back in bed and snoring away before anyone knew he was gone.

It was almost eleven-fifteen when Phoebe was

finally asleep and the light was out under Aunt Daisy's door. George crept out of bed. He quickly got dressed and put his knife in his pocket. He'd need it for prying off the lid of the crate. And who knew? Maybe there was a live cobra in the box too. George could hope, couldn't he?

George opened the door and peeked into the hallway. He wanted to avoid Henry, who seemed to have eyes in the back of his bright orange head. He wouldn't like George creeping around so late at night.

But the hallway was quiet. There was no noise at all except for the quiet hum of the engines, rising up from the bottom of the ship. George loved that noise. It made him think of crickets in the woods at night.

In fact, being out here all by himself reminded him of the nights at home when he sneaked out into the woods while Papa and Phoebe were asleep.

He'd head out when his mind was filled with restless thoughts.

About why Papa was always mad at him, or why he didn't try harder in school.

And of course Mama.

Almost three years had passed since she died. George tried not to think about her too much. But some nights when he closed his eyes, he'd remember her smile. Or her smell when she hugged him close. Like fresh grass and sweet flowers.

And that song she'd sing to wake George up in the morning:

> *"Awake, awake.*
> *It's now daybreak!*
> *But don't forget your dreams. . . ."*

Thinking about Mama was like standing close to a fire. Warm at first. But get too close and it hurt too much.

Much better to stay clear of those thoughts.

Nothing cleared George's mind quicker than being in the woods. He never stayed out for more than an hour or two. . . . Except for that night back in October.

George was heading back toward home when he heard a terrible sound, like a little girl screaming. He turned around, and in the dark distance he saw two glowing yellow eyes.

Some old-timers said there were black panthers in the woods, but George never believed it.

But as the yellow eyes got closer, George could see the outline of a huge cat, with two glistening fangs.

George told himself not to run. He knew he'd never outrun the panther.

But he couldn't help it—he ran as fast as he could. Branches cut his face, but he didn't slow down.

Any second the panther would leap up and tackle George. Its claws would tear him apart.

George could feel the cat right behind him; he could smell its breath, like rotting meat. George grabbed a fallen branch. He turned and waved it in front of him. The panther lunged and grabbed the branch in its jaws.

George let go of the stick and scrambled up a tree, climbing as high as he could go.

The cat dropped the branch and came after him, like a shadow with glowing eyes.

George pulled out his knife.

He waited until the cat's front paws were on the small branch just below him. And then, with all his might, he chopped at the branch with his knife.

Crack.

The branch broke free.

The giant cat tumbled through the air, screaming and crashing through the branches, and then hit the ground with a thud.

There was silence.

And then the cat stood up. It looked up at George for a long moment.

And it turned and walked slowly back into the woods.

George stayed in the tree until it was just about light, and made it into bed just before Papa woke up.

His friends at school refused to believe George when he told them, even when he swore on his heart.

"No way."

"Big fat lie."

"Next thing you'll be saying is that you've been signed by the Giants." Their laughter rose up around George, but it didn't bother him, because right then he realized that it didn't matter what they thought.

George knew he'd faced down the panther.

And he'd never forget it.

CHAPTER 7

Just thinking about seeing the mummy made George happy. He went down five flights of stairs to G deck and practically skipped along the long hallway toward the front of the ship. He ducked into doorways a few times to hide from the night stewards. But he had no trouble finding his way, not like Phoebe, who got lost walking from the dining room to the washroom.

"Next time I'll leave a trail of bread crumbs,

like Hansel and Gretel," she'd said, their first day on board.

"How about lemon drops?" George had suggested.

Phoebe had giggled.

The hold was in the very front of the ship, past the mail sorting room and the cabins where the stokers and firemen stayed. Too bad, George thought, that there wasn't time to sneak in and see the escape ladders. Luckily there were two more days at sea.

George walked right through the doors of the first class baggage room and down a steep metal staircase that led to the hold. All around him were crates and trunks and bags neatly stacked on shelves and lined up on the floor.

It took him a minute to figure out that everything was arranged in alphabetical order, by the owners' names, and a few minutes to find the *B*s.

And there it was, a plain wooden crate stamped with the words:

MR. DAVID BURROWS
NEW YORK CITY
CONTENTS FRAGILE

George smiled to himself.

This was going to be easy.

He took out his knife and started to pry off the lid. He worked carefully, prying each nail loose so he'd be able to close the crate tight again when he was finished.

He'd made it halfway around when he heard a strange sound.

The hair on his arms prickled.

It was the same feeling he'd had the night of the panther, that someone — or something — was watching him.

George stared at the crate, his heart pounding.

And before he could even take a breath, something leaped out of the shadows and pushed him to the ground.

George looked up, half expecting to see a mummy rising out of the crate, her arms reaching for George's throat.

What he saw was almost as horrifying.

It was a man with glittering blue eyes and a scar running down the side of his face.

He grabbed George's knife out of his hand. The man was small, but very strong.

"I'll take this," he said, admiring it. Then he looked George up and down.

"So," the man said. "Trying to fill your pockets with some first class loot?"

George realized he must be a robber. George had caught him in the act!

"Uh, no, I'm . . ."

The man pointed to George's boots. "Which trunk did you steal those from? Cost more than a third class ticket, I'd say."

George shook his head. "I got them in London," he said, and too late realized he'd made a mistake.

"Ah, a prince from first class," the man said with a hearty laugh. "Just down here for a little thrill? What's your name?"

"George," said George softly.

"Prince George," the man said, bowing in a joking way. "A pity those boots wouldn't fit me," he added, standing up. "But you do have something I'd like. Your key. Always wanted to see one of those first class cabins."

There was no way George could let this man up to the suite! He'd jump overboard before he let him near Aunt Daisy and Phoebe.

"There's a mummy down here!" he blurted out. "It's worth millions! It's in that crate!"

The man raised an eyebrow.

George kept talking.

"I thought I could sneak it off the ship and sell it in New York," George lied. "My father's business is bad. I thought if I could sell it . . ."

The man looked at the crate.

"I like the way you think," he said.

He waved the knife at George and told him not to move. And then he quickly worked the knife around the lid. Obviously he'd done this many times before.

He lifted the lid off the crate. But before either of them could look inside, there was a tremendous rumbling noise, and the entire hold began to shake so hard that George almost fell. The shaking got stronger and stronger, the noise louder and louder, like thunder exploding all around them. A trunk tumbled off a shelf and hit the scar-faced man on the head. The knife clattered to the floor, but George didn't try to get it. Here was his chance to escape. He spun around, ran up the stairs, and darted out the door.

CHAPTER 8

George ran as fast as he could down the hall. He heard shouting behind him, but he didn't stop until he was back on B deck, safe again in first class.

A steward hurried past him with a stack of clean towels.

"Good evening, sir," he said.

George nodded, out of breath.

Nothing could happen to him up here, he knew. So why was his heart still pounding?

It was the ship, he realized — that thundering noise. That shaking in the hold. Had a boiler exploded? Had a steam pipe burst?

An eerie silence surrounded him, and George's heart skipped a beat as he realized that the engines had been turned off. The quiet rumbling had stopped.

Just outside, George heard people talking loudly. Did they know what was happening?

George went out onto the deck and walked over to the small crowd of men. Most were still dressed in their dinner tuxedos and puffing on cigars. They were standing at the rail, pointing and laughing at something happening on the well deck, one level below. What was so funny?

George squeezed between two men and looked over the rail.

At first he was sure his eyes were playing tricks. It looked like the well deck had been through a winter storm. It was covered with ice and slush. A bunch of young men in tattered coats and hats were pelting each other with balls of ice, roaring with laughter like kids having a snowball fight.

"What's happened?" asked a man who'd walked up behind George.

"The ship nudged an iceberg!" said an old man with a bushy mustache. He didn't sound worried.

An iceberg!

"Is that why they've stopped the engines?" said the new man. "Because of some ice on the deck?"

"Just being cautious, it seems, following regulations," said the older fellow. "I spoke to one of the officers. He assured me we'll be underway any moment. Hey there!" he yelled down to the young men below. "Toss some of that ice up here!"

One of the gang picked up a piece of ice the size of a baseball. He threw it, but the man with the bushy mustache missed. George reached out and made a clean catch with one hand. The crowd cheered. George held up the ice and smiled. Then he held it out to the man.

"Keep it, son!" he said. "There's plenty for everyone."

The piece of ice was heavier than George had expected.

He sniffed it and wrinkled his nose.

It smelled like old sardines!

More ice balls came sailing up from below, and the men jostled to catch them.

Their laughter and cheers rose up around George, and the fear he'd felt in the baggage hold faded away. From up here, on the deck of this incredible ship, George felt powerful. Nothing could hurt him on the *Titanic*.

Not a meteor falling from space. Not a giant squid.

Not the scar-faced man.

George squinted out into the distance, hoping to see the iceberg, but the sea faded into darkness.

His teeth were chattering now. It was so much

colder than it had been at dinnertime. He wanted to be back in bed, curled up under his fancy first class sheets and blankets.

The corridor was still quiet as George crept toward his suite.

As he was letting himself in, he stepped on something that made a crunching sound under his boot. At first George thought that it was ice or a piece of glass. But when he picked up his heel, he saw that the carpet was covered with yellow crystals.

George smiled. It was just one of Phoebe's lemon drops.

George let himself in, easing the door shut.

Phoebe's bed curtains were closed. The light under Aunt Daisy's door was off.

George quickly changed into his pajamas and climbed into bed.

Yes, he was safe, he told himself.

He tried to go to sleep, but as the minutes ticked by, his mind got restless.

It hit him that his knife was gone, forever, and the total silence of the ship seemed to press down on him. Why hadn't the engines started up again?

He lay wide awake, listening and wondering.

It was almost a relief when he heard someone knocking on their door.

CHAPTER 9

It was Henry.

"Hello, George," said Henry. "Can I speak to Mrs. Key, please?"

Henry wore his usual polite smile, but his voice wasn't jolly.

"What is it?" said Aunt Daisy, stepping out of her room.

"So sorry to barge in like this, ma'am," Henry said. "But there's been an . . . incident."

Aunt Daisy glared at George.

"I'm so sorry, Henry," she said in an exasperated voice. "My nephew here just can't seem to stay out of trouble!"

"Oh, no, ma'am!" Henry exclaimed. "This has nothing to do with George. It's the ship, ma'am. Seems we've bumped an iceberg. I'm sure the captain is just being cautious, but he wants everyone up on deck."

"It's after midnight," Aunt Daisy said with a laugh. "Surely the captain doesn't expect us to appear on deck in our nightclothes!"

"No, ma'am. It's very cold outside." Henry walked over to the dresser and brought out three life jackets. "And you'll need to put these on. Over your coats."

Aunt Daisy stared at the life jackets as if Henry was holding up clown costumes.

"Henry! I'm not taking the children out into the cold for some kind of drill! Has Captain Smith lost his senses?"

"Of course not, Mrs. Key," Henry said. "Now

if you could get yourself and the children ready. I'll be back in just a moment to see if you need any help."

He left them alone.

"All right, George," Aunt Daisy said. "I guess we'll have another adventure to boast about when we get back. You get dressed. I'll get Phoebe up."

Aunt Daisy went to Phoebe's bed, pulling aside the curtains.

George heard a gasp, and he rushed over.

Phoebe wasn't there.

"Where could she be?" Aunt Daisy exclaimed.

A cold feeling crept up George's spine. Phoebe, his guardian angel. She must have woken up while George was gone, and now she was somewhere on the ship. Searching for George.

He took a deep breath.

"I went out exploring," George said. "After you went to bed. I didn't think Phoebe would wake up. She never does!"

"So she's out there looking for you?" Aunt Daisy said.

George nodded. "She doesn't want me getting into trouble." He kept his eyes glued to the floor. Aunt Daisy should be furious with him, and Papa was right! George had no sense. Not one lick of sense.

How would they ever find Phoebe?

But then George had an idea . . . that lemon drop in the hallway.

Could it be?

He ran out into the corridor, which was still empty. It seemed Henry wasn't having much luck getting people out of bed and up onto the deck.

George ran a little ways down the hall.

There!

He hurried down a bit farther.

Yes! Another lemon drop!

Phoebe! His smart sister!

Aunt Daisy came up behind him.

"She's left a trail of lemon drops," George said.

Aunt Daisy looked confused.

"Like Hansel and Gretel," George explained. "She left a trail so she could find her way back."

CHAPTER 10

George and Aunt Daisy scrambled to get dressed
and put on their life jackets. Aunt Daisy brought
Phoebe's warmest coat, and George carried the
extra life jacket. They'd quickly find Phoebe
and head up to the boat deck. And tomorrow
morning this would be a big joke to laugh at over
breakfast.

George thought that Phoebe had gone to the
promenade deck — that she'd been woken up

by the commotion with the ice and figured that George had gone out to see what was happening.

But when they got to the main staircase, he saw that the yellow glints were headed downstairs, not up to the deck.

His heart sank.

Phoebe had headed down to the first class baggage hold. Because she knew that George would want to see that mummy.

Of course she'd known.

Phoebe could read his mind.

A chill went through George's bones.

What if the scar-faced man was lurking in the baggage hold when Phoebe got there?

He ran faster down the stairs now. Aunt Daisy called after him, but he didn't slow down.

But when he got down to G deck, there was a gate stretched across the doorway.

"This wasn't here when I came down," he said to Aunt Daisy. He tried to pull it open, but it was locked. And just on the other side there was

a mob of people standing restlessly, third class passengers from the looks of their worn clothing.

"Look," Aunt Daisy said, pointing at one of Phoebe's candies glinting on the floor on the other side of the gate, pushed next to the wall. "She's down here. Pardon me!" she called to the steward standing in front of the crowd.

"You've gone the wrong way, madam," he said, staring at Aunt Daisy's huge diamond ring. "The captain wants first class passengers up on the boat deck now."

"My niece is down here somewhere," Aunt Daisy said. "You need to let us through."

"I'm sure she wouldn't have wandered down this far," the steward said.

"We're quite sure she's down here," Aunt Daisy said. "So if you'll please open the gate."

"I'm sorry, madam," he said. "Regulations . . ."

"Open this gate at once!" Aunt Daisy shouted in a tone George had never heard her use before.

The man took a key from his pocket and opened the gate. He stepped aside to let them pass. The crowd surged forward.

"Get back!" the steward shouted. "We'll tell you when it's time for you to go up!"

A few of the men lunged toward him.

Aunt Daisy grabbed George's arm.

The steward took a pistol from his pocket. His hand shook as he waved it toward the crowd. George and Aunt Daisy stepped through the gate. The steward slammed it behind them.

They were trapped down there, just like everyone else.

George and Aunt Daisy squeezed through the crowd, weaving around trunks and stepping over sleeping children. There were so many people. If Phoebe's candies were down here, they couldn't see them anymore.

Suddenly something crashed into George from behind. A pair of arms wrapped around his waist so tightly he couldn't breathe.

George's heart stopped—the scar-faced man?

"GIORGIO!" Enzo screamed up at him.

George's eardrums nearly split in two.

Enzo's father hurried over to them. He tried to gently peel Enzo away from George.

But the little boy wouldn't let go.

"NO!" he howled. "NO!"

"Very sorry," Marco said, smiling apologetically at Aunt Daisy, who looked more confused than ever. "We are old friends of Giorgio."

George started to introduce Aunt Daisy, but before he could get three words out, Enzo was dragging him down the hall, elbowing his way through the crowd like a pint-sized bull.

"See! See!" Enzo said.

"What?" George said. "No . . ."

"See! See!"

What was this kid doing? What did he want George to see?

The answer was just a few steps away, through an open doorway.

It was the mail sorting room.

Except now all George could see was water, green water swirling halfway up the stairs, foaming and churning like a stormy river. Sacks of mail bobbed up and down. Hundreds of letters floated on the surface.

And now George understood what Enzo was saying.

Sea.

The sea.

The *Titanic* was filling with water from the sea.

CHAPTER 11

Unsinkable.

Unsinkable.

George whispered those words like a prayer, over and over in his mind. He thought of Mr. Andrews, of how sure he was of this ship.

But the longer he stared at that water, that foaming green water, rising higher every second, the more certain he became: The *Titanic* was in trouble.

"We must go up," Marco said to Aunt Daisy. "We find a way."

But she shook her head, holding up Phoebe's bright blue coat and her life jacket.

"My niece, Phoebe," Aunt Daisy said. "She's down here. . . ."

George could see she was fighting back tears. George had never seen her look so sad and helpless, not even when Uncle Cliff died.

"She came down here looking for me," George said. "We can't find her."

Marco's amber eyes became very intent.

"An idea," he said. He knelt down and spoke to Enzo in Italian.

The boy smiled and nodded.

Then Marco hoisted the little boy up onto his shoulders.

Enzo took a huge breath and screamed,

"Phoebe!

"PHOEBE!"

People stopped talking and stared up at the boy with the foghorn voice.

"Phoebe!

"PHOEBE!"

As a hush fell over the crowd, George heard a faint voice.

"I'm here! I'm here!"

The crowd parted, and Phoebe appeared, her spectacles crooked, her face pale.

She staggered forward and threw her arms around George, burying her face in his chest.

"I found you," she whispered.

George didn't bother arguing over who did the finding. And anyway, his words were stuck in his throat. So he just held her tight.

It took some time for Phoebe to calm down enough to tell her story: that yes, she had been looking for George and heading for the baggage hold, that she got caught in the crowd of people rushing toward the back of the ship.

"It was like a stampede," she said.

As Phoebe talked, Aunt Daisy helped her into her coat and life jacket. Enzo held Phoebe's hand, like they were old friends. And the strange thing was that it felt that way, like they'd known Marco and Enzo forever. Maybe that's what happened when you got trapped in a flooding ship together.

George started to feel calmer with Phoebe close to him.

But then came a deep booming sound, a kind of groaning that echoed up all around them. At first George thought maybe the engines had started up again. But no, this wasn't the sound of the *Titanic*'s mighty engines.

The entire ship catapulted forward. People fell, toppling like dominoes. George was thrown into the wall. Screams and shouts echoed through the hallway. He managed to grab Enzo by the life jacket as he went sailing by him. Enzo just giggled as he fell into George's lap. To him this was a fun game. George hoped he never figured out that it wasn't.

"What was that?" Phoebe gasped, digging her fingers into George's arms.

Nobody answered.

But they all knew.

The *Titanic* was sinking.

"We will go up," Marco said.

"How?" Aunt Daisy said.

Phoebe grabbed George's hand.

"You, Georgie," she said.

"What?" George said.

"Phoebe's right," Aunt Daisy said. "You know the ship better than anyone." She turned to Marco. "He's explored every inch."

George couldn't believe it. They were counting on him?

But what if he made a mistake?

What if they all got lost?

"You can do it," Phoebe whispered.

And so George closed his eyes, picturing Mr. Andrews's blueprints in his mind.

And he remembered: the escape ladders.

He remembered what Mr. Andrews had told him: *The ladders are in the stokers' quarters, and they run up three decks.*

He pointed toward the front of the ship.

"This way," he said.

CHAPTER 12

There was no crowd here. Just abandoned trunks and suitcases.

And water. It was seeping into the hallway from under the doors of some of the cabins. No wonder those people were trying to push their way upstairs. They'd probably known right away that the ship was in trouble and the bottom decks were flooding.

The door to the stokers' quarters was locked.

Marco handed Enzo over to George and rammed the door with his shoulder, breaking the lock.

George rushed inside and went to the back wall.

And there it was, a ladder bolted to the wall. Just like Mr. Andrews said it would be. It came through the floor and shot straight up through an opening in the ceiling. George almost laughed with relief.

"Bravo, George!" Marco said.

"Bravo, Giorgio!" Enzo said, clapping.

George hopped up onto the ladder, with Phoebe and Aunt Daisy at his heels.

George was worried about Enzo, but the little guy scrambled like a monkey right ahead of Marco. They came up in a small dining room meant for crew members, and then George led everyone down a long second class corridor, up the grand staircase, and finally out onto the crowded boat deck.

They'd made it!

An officer came hurrying over to Aunt Daisy.

"Madam, there is a lifeboat about to leave. You and the children must come at once."

The man looked at Marco.

"Women and children only, sir," he said somberly. "I'm afraid you will have to stay with the other gentlemen."

Marco nodded. "Yes," he said. "I know."

Phoebe had been right. There weren't enough lifeboats. Not nearly enough.

What would happen to all of these men on deck? There were hundreds of them! And what about the crew? And those people down on G deck?

George's heart was pounding so hard he thought it would break through his chest.

He felt dizzy and sick.

Marco got down on his knees and spoke very quietly to Enzo.

Enzo nodded. Marco kissed him on the forehead, and then Enzo ran over to Aunt Daisy. She picked him up.

"I say he will go on a special boat ride," Marco said. "I say you will not leave him."

Aunt Daisy nodded, her eyes welling with tears.

"I promise you that."

Marco and Aunt Daisy looked at each other. Neither of them said a word, but a whole conversation seemed to happen with their eyes.

Phoebe was really crying now, looking away so Enzo wouldn't see. George felt like someone was choking him.

"Come on now!" the officer screamed.

And so they left Marco, and when George turned around just a few seconds later, he was gone.

The officer led them through a crowd of men to the side of the ship, where a lifeboat hung just over the side. It was packed with people, all women and children except for two sailors who stood at either end.

An officer helped Phoebe over the rail, and then one of the sailors reached over and pulled her into the boat. George helped Enzo, who tumbled in next to Phoebe. Aunt Daisy had a hard time climbing over in her skirts, but George held her hand, and she finally made it.

Now it was George's turn. As he took a step over the railing, someone pulled him back roughly.

"No more room," the officer said. "Women and children only. Lower away!" he called.

"No!" called Aunt Daisy, standing up in the boat. "He's only ten years old! Wait!"

The lifeboat rocked and almost tipped over. Ladies shrieked.

"You will drown us all!" a woman shouted.

"Sit down or I'll throw you over!" the sailor said.

And now Phoebe was screaming too.

Enzo howled.

George was too shocked to move.

Phoebe leaped up and grabbed hold of one of the ropes. She was trying to climb out of the lifeboat, back to George. He gasped as her hand slipped and she dangled over the sea. A sailor grabbed her around the waist and threw her into the boat.

And then the boat slid down on its ropes and splashed into the water.

Aunt Daisy and Phoebe were shouting up at him as the sailors rowed the boat away. George stood there at the rail, watching, his entire body shaking.

He stood there for what felt like a long time after their boat disappeared into the darkness.

He couldn't look down at the water, so he stared up at the sky, at all of those stars.

He closed his eyes and told himself it was a nightmare. He was really asleep in his suite. Or no, he was home on the farm, in his bed, with

Phoebe sleeping across the room and Papa sitting by the fire downstairs.

He closed his eyes tighter.

He tried to block out the terrible noises around him. He felt himself tipping to the side and he held tighter to the rail. And then he couldn't hold on anymore. His hand slipped.

And George fell, smashing his head on the deck.

And then there was silence.

CHAPTER 13

Strong arms lifted George up. He felt himself being carried.

"Papa?" he said. "Papa?"

Why did his head hurt so much? Had the panther knocked him out of the tree? Was he sick with a fever like Mama? And whose voice was whispering in his ear?

"Giorgio. Giorgio. Wake up."

George opened his eyes. Marco's amber eyes shone down on him.

This was no dream. He was not sick.

The *Titanic* was sinking.

The bow was completely underwater now, and waves swept over the deck. Lounge chairs sailed past them and crashed over the side. People clung to the rails. A few slipped and were swept overboard.

Marco had wrapped one arm around the railing and the other around George.

"It's time to go," Marco said.

"Go where?" George said, even though he knew.

They were going into the water. There was nowhere else for them to go.

Marco held George's arm as they climbed over the railing.

"When we jump, jump as far out as you can," Marco said. "Away from the ship."

George filled his lungs with the icy air.

"Jump!" Marco cried.

George pushed with his feet and leaped off the

boat. He closed his eyes, imagining that he had enormous wings that would take him soaring into the sky.

But then he hit the water, and down he went.

And just when he was sure his lungs would pop, the ocean seemed to spit him back up. George sputtered. The water was so cold it felt like millions of needles were stabbing him. It hurt so much he couldn't move.

Someone grabbed him by the life jacket and started dragging him away from the ship. It took George a few seconds to realize that it was Marco. He stopped to grab a door that was floating by. After helping George climb up on top, Marco found a crate for himself. It wasn't big enough to keep his feet out of the water. But it was better than nothing. The crate had a rope attached to it. Marco tied it around his arm and handed the end to George.

"Hold tight," he said.

They turned and stared at the ship.

The entire front was underwater, and the back had risen toward the sky. It groaned and squeaked and sparked. Black smoke poured from its funnels, and the lights flickered. It was like watching a fairy-tale dragon, stabbed and bleeding, fighting for its life.

And finally it seemed to give up.

The groaning stopped. The lights went dark. And the *Titanic* sank into the bubbling black water, down, down, down, down, until George closed his eyes.

He couldn't make himself watch Mr. Andrews's beautiful ship disappear.

A sound rose up around him, people calling for help. More and more people, screaming and yelling, hundreds of voices swirling together like a howling wind.

Marco pulled George away from the people and the wreckage. George couldn't believe how

strong he was, how hard he kicked, how his arms sliced through the water.

When he finally stopped, Marco was gasping for breath, exhaling cold clouds of white mist. He tightened the rope around his arm and patted George on the shoulder.

"I rest now, Giorgio," he said breathlessly. He closed his eyes and put his head down on the crate. "Soon."

Soon what? George was afraid to ask. Soon it would be over? Soon they would be rescued? Or soon they would be swallowed up by the darkness?

George heard men talking somewhere close by.

He looked around, relieved that he wasn't all by himself, and to his shock, just ahead, he saw a lifeboat.

"Marco!" he said. "Wake up!"

But Marco didn't move. His arms hung off the side of the crate. His feet dangled in the icy water.

"Marco! We need to get to that boat!"

But Marco was still. And George realized that his friend had used every last ounce of strength. He'd gotten George off the sinking ship, and across the icy waters.

It was up to George now.

He tucked the rope under his body and started paddling. The water seared his hands and arms. It was so cold it felt boiling hot, like lava.

But he didn't stop until he reached the boat.

It wasn't a regular wooden lifeboat. It was much smaller, and made of canvas cloth. There were about ten people crowded inside, mostly men. They all seemed dazed and frozen. Nobody spoke as George paddled up and grabbed hold of the side.

But somebody pushed his hand off.

"Get back," a voice said weakly. "You'll put us all in the water."

"Please," George said. "We need help."

George put his hand up again, but again someone pushed it off.

And so George pulled Marco to the other side of the boat. He tried again.

Nobody helped him. But this time nobody stopped him.

It took him three tries, but he managed to hoist himself over the side and tumble into the boat.

And now for Marco.

He got up on his knees and leaned over, bracing his legs against the side of the boat as he grabbed Marco under the arms. He pulled, but Marco was attached to the crate by the rope. He tried again, yanking the rope, digging at the knot with his frozen fingers. But the knot was like rusted metal. George struggled, and water sloshed over the side of the boat.

"Just let him go," one of the men said weakly. "It's hopeless."

But George kept working on the rope, trying now to break it away from the crate. He was pulling so hard that at first he didn't notice that Marco was slipping into the sea.

"Please! Somebody!" George screamed. "Can't you help us?"

A woman from the front of the boat climbed back to George.

She wore a black coat, her head and face hidden by a flowered shawl. As she pushed George aside she pulled something out of her coat.

A knife!

With a clean cut, she sliced the rope and helped George pull Marco into the boat.

Her hands looked surprisingly strong.

George fell back, exhausted.

"Thank you," George said to the woman through his chattering teeth.

The woman didn't say anything, and suddenly George noticed the knife. A bowie knife with an elk-horn handle.

George looked up, under the shawl. Two glittering blue eyes looked back at him.

The scar-faced man.

He had saved Marco's life.

Without a word, he handed George his knife.

Then he looked away.

CHAPTER 14

The cold pressed down on George until it seemed to crush his bones. He huddled close to Marco, trying to keep them both warm. Marco barely moved.

Some of the men sang softly.

Others prayed.

Some made no sounds at all.

Hours went by.

The sea became rougher, and every few minutes a wave splashed into the boat.

George was drifting off to sleep when one of the men shouted.

"It's a ship!"

And sure enough, a bright light was heading toward them.

"No," another man said. "It's just lightning."

But the light was getting bigger. And brighter.

George stared at that light, afraid that if he even blinked it would disappear, but soon he could see the outline of a gigantic ship steaming toward them.

He whispered to Marco, who barely fluttered his eyes. He pulled his friend closer, rubbing his arms.

"It won't be long," he whispered. "Hang on."

As the sky brightened, George gaped at the scene around him. It was as if they'd fallen through a hole in the ocean and come out on the other side of the earth.

There were icebergs all around them — hundreds of them, as far as George could see.

They sparkled in the golden pink light. They were so beautiful, but looking at them sent a chill up George's spine.

As the ship got closer, George could see that it was a passenger steamer, like the *Titanic*. Closer and closer it came, until George could read its name: *Carpathia*.

There were people crowded on the deck, looking over the rail. They were yelling and shouting and waving. But one voice rose above all the others, like a siren:

"PAPA! PAPA! GIORGIO!"

Marco's eyes fluttered, and he smiled a little.

"Enzo," he whispered.

George could see the little boy, waving frantically from Aunt Daisy's arms. Phoebe stood next to them, waving, with the sunlight glinting off her spectacles.

"They're safe, Marco!" George said. "They made it!"

George grabbed Marco's hand.

"And so did we."

CHAPTER 15

Those first two days on the *Carpathia* were a blur.

George mostly slept, on a bed of blankets and pillows on the floor of the first class lounge. But he sensed that Phoebe and Aunt Daisy never left his side. He sometimes heard Enzo singing softly to him in Italian, his breath hot on George's cheek. He heard Aunt Daisy and Phoebe talking—about Marco, whose feet were badly frozen, about the *Carpathia*'s passengers, who couldn't do enough for them all. About the hundreds and hundreds of people who didn't make it out of the water.

Slowly George felt stronger, and on their last night at sea, he was able to go out onto the deck with Phoebe.

They sat on a bench, wrapped in a blanket. A stewardess came over and gave them each a mug of warm milk.

Phoebe looked up at the sky as she warmed her hands on her mug.

"I finally saw a shooting star, when I was on the lifeboat," she said. "You can guess what I wished for."

George reached for her hand.

Yes, of course he knew.

On the bench next to them sat two women. Both were crying. Probably they'd lost their husbands. Or brothers. Or fathers.

There hadn't been enough wishing stars for everyone that night.

Phoebe said that only about 700 of them made it out of the water.

Phoebe leaned in close to George. Her coat smelled like rose water. A lady from the *Carpathia* had given it to her.

"Have you wondered?" she asked quietly, "if maybe there really was a curse?"

At first George didn't understand that Phoebe was talking about the mummy.

With all that had happened, George hadn't thought about it.

But now it hit him: how strange it was that the ship had collided with the iceberg at the exact moment the scar-faced man had opened the lid of Mr. Burrows's crate.

"I guess we'll never know," George said.

But the next evening, as the *Carpathia* was closing in on New York Harbor, George and Phoebe overheard a skinny man with a beard speaking to an officer.

"Before the *Titanic*, I was traveling in Egypt, a

place called Thebes," the man said. "I explored a magnificent tomb of a royal family."

Phoebe's eyes bugged out.

And before George could stop her, she had marched over to the man.

"Excuse me," she said. "Are you Mr. Burrows?"

"Yes, I am," the man replied.

Phoebe took a big breath.

"Mr. Burrows," she said. "This might sound like a very strange question. But did you bring a mummy on board the *Titanic*?"

The man looked at Phoebe.

"A mummy?" he said.

"Yes," she said. "We heard it was a princess."

Mr. Burrows's eyes were tired and sad.

But he smiled a little.

"My princess," he said. "Yes."

"So there *was* a mummy?" Phoebe exclaimed.

"No, child," he said. "One should never take a mummy from a tomb. That is very bad luck.

Princess was my cat. She passed away on my trip to Egypt. And so I had her . . . wrapped, so I could bring her back with me."

"So the princess was a cat?"

"Yes," he said sadly. "The most beautiful cat that ever lived."

Three hours later, just after nine o'clock, the *Carpathia* docked in New York City in a thunderstorm.

There were thousands of people waiting on the pier.

But the first person George saw as they walked down the gangplank was Papa. He rushed up to George and Phoebe, grabbing them both and pulling them to him. All around them, people cried with happiness. Others just cried, their tears mixing with the pouring rain.

They introduced Papa to Marco and Enzo, but there wasn't much time to talk. Their train to

Millerstown was leaving soon, and an ambulance was waiting to take Marco to the hospital.

Luckily, George didn't have to say a real good-bye to Marco and Enzo.

Aunt Daisy was staying in New York City to take care of Enzo until Marco's feet were healed. And then they would come with her for a visit to Millerstown. Seeing the way Marco and Aunt Daisy were looking at each other, George wondered if maybe Marco and Enzo would stay forever. George sure hoped so.

As they rode to the train station, newsboys screamed from every street corner.

"Read all about it! Titanic *survivors in New York! More than fifteen hundred people dead! Read all about it!"*

George covered his ears.

He wanted to forget everything about the *Titanic*.

He wanted to put it out of his mind forever.

CHAPTER 16

But he couldn't forget.

Even back on the farm, surrounded by friends from school and neighbors from town, he felt like he was still drifting on the dark ocean. And each day that went by, he felt himself drifting farther away. At night, when he got into bed, he'd see the faces of all those scared people on G deck. He'd see the ship disappearing into the sea. He'd remember the stabbing cold, and the screams of hundreds of people crying for help.

He didn't bother trying to fall asleep. Each night, after Phoebe and Papa were in bed, he went out into the woods.

He was heading back to the house one night when he heard a noise through the bushes.

Something was there. He could sense it.

The panther?

He took out his knife, fighting the urge to run away, and peered through the branches.

George stared in shock.

It was Papa.

He was sitting on a large rock, looking up at the sky, smoking his pipe. He looked like he'd been there for some time.

Papa turned. He didn't look especially surprised to see George.

"Sorry to give you a scare," he said.

"What are you doing here?" George asked.

"Don't know," Papa said. "Sometimes I just come here, when I can't sleep."

George couldn't believe it. How many nights

had they both been out in the woods at the same time?

Papa eased himself off the rock and began walking back toward the house. "I'll take you up to your bed."

"No, Papa," George said. "I come to the woods too."

Papa looked at him with a very slight smile.

"I know that," he said.

Papa knew? What else did Papa know about George?

What else *didn't* George know about Papa?

He and and his father looked at each other. Really looked, for the first time in a long while, maybe since Mama died.

Suddenly George started to cry. They took him by surprise, his tears, and he couldn't stop. He cried for all those people who didn't make it out of the water. He cried because somehow he did. He cried because he knew that no matter how much time went by, a part of him would still be out in that ocean. He would never forget.

Papa held George's hand and didn't say a word. And then he led George over to the boulder, where they sat together under the stars.

George stared up at the sky. Were those really the same stars that had burned so brightly above the black ocean that night?

Was he really still the same boy?

George, who couldn't stay out of trouble. George, who didn't try hard at school.

George, who found the escape ladders. George, who pulled Marco to that lifeboat.

Who didn't give up.

They sat on the boulder for a long while, and as the sun started to peep over the trees, George told Papa about Mr. Andrews.

"He said he thought one day I'd build a ship."

Papa didn't laugh. He puffed on his pipe, looking thoughtful.

"How about we build one together?" Papa said. "A nice little boat. For the pond. I've always wanted to do that."

"That's a good idea," George said.

A great idea.

"We could start today," Papa said, standing up and holding out his hand.

They walked back to the house together. The birds were singing softly. The chickens were squawking for breakfast. A breeze was whispering through the trees. And a voice seemed to sing to George, very softly:

> *"Awake, awake.*
> *It's now daybreak!*
> *But don't forget your dreams. . . ."*

Papa looked out into the woods, like he could hear it too.

MY *TITANIC* STORY

This book is a work of historical fiction. That means that all of the facts about the *Titanic* are true, but the main characters came from my imagination. George, Phoebe, Aunt Daisy, Marco, and Enzo are based on people I learned about while researching the *Titanic*. By the time I finished writing this book, they sure felt real to me.

I can see George now, relaxing in the little boat he and Papa built, rowing around their pond while Phoebe watches from the shore, reading a book about dinosaur fossils. I can picture Aunt Daisy and Marco's wedding, how Enzo would run down the aisle with a huge grin on his face. That's my favorite part of being a writer, giving my characters happiness in the end. If only I could do the same for the 1,517 people who didn't survive the sinking of the *Titanic*.

What a sad and terrible story!

One day as I was trying to finish the book, I needed a break, so I went to New York City with my eleven-year-old son, Dylan. We stopped to rest in one of my favorite neighborhoods, in a tiny park on West 106th Street and Broadway with trees and a bronze statue of a woman lying on her side. I read the gold writing engraved in a marble bench, and to my surprise I saw that the entire park was a memorial to two famous New Yorkers who died on the *Titanic*, Isidor and Ida Straus.

I couldn't forget the *Titanic*, it seemed, not even for an afternoon.

And nearly one hundred years later, the world hasn't forgotten either.

Lauren Tarshis

FACTS ABOUT THE *TITANIC*

More has been written about the *Titanic* than any other disaster in modern history. I tried to include as much information as I could in the book. But here are some more amazing facts that I wanted to share with you.

- The *Titanic* was the largest ship—the largest moving object—ever built. It weighed close to 50,000 tons, and was eleven stories tall and four city blocks long.

- There were 2,229 people on board—1,316 passengers and 913 crew. Survivors included 498 passengers and 215 members of the crew.

- The passengers came from 28 different countries, including many from America, England, Ireland, and

Finland. There were a few passengers from China, Japan, Mexico, and South Africa. Most of the crew members were from England and Ireland.

- There were nine dogs on the *Titanic*. They stayed in kennels, but their owners could take them out onto the decks for walks. Two Pomeranians and one Pekingese survived with their masters.

- After the sinking of the *Titanic*, laws were changed to require all ships to carry enough lifeboats for every passenger and crew member.

- For decades, divers, scientists, and treasure hunters searched for the wreck of the *Titanic*. It was finally located in 1985 by a team led by U.S. scientist Robert Ballard, 2 1/2 miles below the surface of the sea.

- Ballard and his team did not take anything from the wreck. Dr. Ballard believes the *Titanic* should rest in peace as a memorial to those who died. But he couldn't stop treasure hunters from diving to the wreck and removing thousands of artifacts: jewelry, dishes, clothes, even the ship's hull.

What do you think about this? Do you think the *Titanic* should be brought to the surface or left in peace?

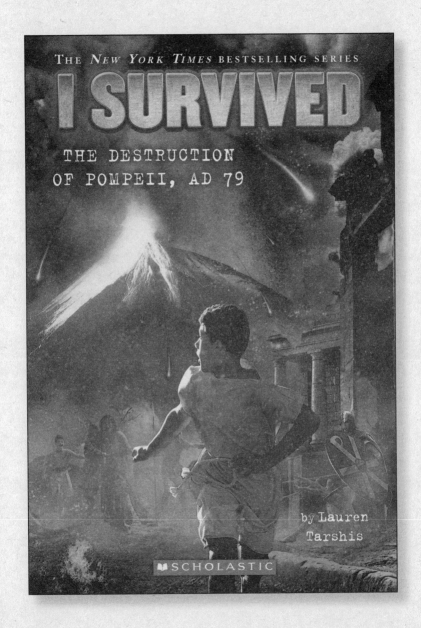

I SURVIVED

THE DESTRUCTION OF POMPEII, AD 79

by Lauren Tarshis

illustrated by Scott Dawson

Scholastic Inc.

CHAPTER 1

AUGUST 24, AD 79
1:00 P.M.
THE CITY OF POMPEII
THE ROMAN EMPIRE

Within hours, thousands of people would be dead.

The entire city of Pompeii would vanish under more than thirty feet of fiery ash and stone.

But first, it was a bright, sunny summer day. Shops bustled. Kids played ball in a grassy field. Gladiators readied for a bloody match.

Nobody yet knew that the mountain Vesuvius, which loomed over the city, was actually a deadly volcano. The mountain had been silent for centuries, a giant green triangle covered with farms and meadows and forests.

It was impossible to imagine what lurked under the ground — rivers of boiling magma, swirls of poisonous gases. Any moment, the mountain would erupt with devastating fury.

Eleven-year-old Marcus was with his father, Tata. They shouldn't have been anywhere near Pompeii. They were escaped slaves, running for their lives from evil men.

But then:

BOOM!

BOOM!

With two shattering explosions, Vesuvius erupted.

Thousands of pairs of eyes turned toward the mountain, staring in shock and terror. Black, billowing smoke and ash gushed out of the mountain's gaping mouth. Vesuvius roared like a furious beast, breathing smoke and flames into the sky. And then came an even bigger cloud, shooting out billions of hot, jagged rocks that rained down on Pompeii, filling fountains, crushing roofs, and pounding down on people as they tried to flee, screaming in panic.

"*The gods are punishing us!*"

"*The world is ending!*"

Marcus and Tata knew they had to escape. Any minute a flaming wave of ash and gases would rush down the mountain, burning everything in its path. But there were too many people in the streets, too many rocks falling from the sky. It was hard to breathe, almost impossible to see. And then there was the strange whooshing sound that came from above.

"Look out!" Tata shouted.

Marcus looked up just in time to see a massive flaming boulder falling from the sky, a chunk of fiery rock from deep inside the mountain.

It was heading right for them.

CHAPTER 2

AUGUST 23, AD 79
THE AFTERNOON BEFORE
MAIN STREET, POMPEII

Marcus walked along the dusty main street of Pompeii, carrying a smelly sack stuffed with his master's dirty laundry. It was early afternoon, and the street was packed with people — shoppers sifting through bins of pomegranates and melons, weary slaves collecting water from the fountains, beggars holding out their grimy hands.

A snake charmer dozed while his cobra peeked out of its basket, tasting the air with its flicking tongue.

"Salve," Marcus said, a friendly Latin hello for the deadly reptile. If only he had a basket to hide in right now. There were no good days for Marcus lately, but this day was sure to be more miserable than usual.

It was broiling hot and his ragged tunic was soaked in sweat. Even worse, his master, Festus Julius, was expecting important guests from Rome this evening, friends of the emperor. This meant even more backbreaking work than usual for Marcus and the other slaves. For days they'd been scrubbing the villa so that the mosaic floors shined like diamonds, so that every silver bowl and goblet gleamed.

The guests would arrive by chariot — men in flowing white togas, women in silk robes and with painted red lips, jewels flashing from every finger. Tonight there would be a great feast of roasted flamingo and wild boar, honey-baked mice stuffed with raisins and dates, and lobsters as big as cats. The guests would lounge on silken couches and gorge themselves until they threw up . . . and then, their stomachs empty, they would eat more.

Tomorrow, Festus would take them all to the gladiator fight at Pompeii's amphitheater. From front-row seats, they would cheer as the warriors tried to stab one another to death with swords, spears, and daggers.

People were coming from all over to see the spectacle, which featured Pompeii's champion fighter. He was a giant of a man, who had lost an eye in one of his early battles. The injury had earned him the fighting name of Cyclops, after the one-eyed monster from the old Greek tales. Like almost all gladiators, Cyclops was a slave who was forced to fight. But he was one of the lucky few — still alive after many battles.

Just thinking about these brutal tournaments horrified Marcus.

Suddenly his whole body was shaking.

But wait, it wasn't Marcus who was trembling.

It was the earth beneath his feet!

Marcus dropped his sack and braced himself against a stone fountain. A huge marble statue of the warrior Achilles looked down on him.

Marcus wished he felt as brave as Achilles!

But these tremors spooked him. For weeks they'd been shaking the city, putting cracks in the walls of Festus's villa, sending his spoiled dogs into fits of howling.

Usually the quakes were quick, ending in just a few seconds. Most people seemed to barely notice them.

But this quake was more powerful than most.

The ground shuddered and shook, harder and harder.

Up and down the street, the sound of shattering glass and splintering wood and crumbling stone pounded Marcus's ears.

Crash!

Crack!

Bang!

Vendors cursed as their baskets of fruit and vegetables toppled. A bamboo birdcage fell and burst open, scattering a flock of tiny white birds into the dusty air. Barrels rolled wildly through the streets, gushing wine as red as blood.

Marcus held tight to the fountain as the water inside it sloshed, splashing over the rim and soaking his tunic.

And then he heard it, a creaking just over his head. Marcus looked up just as the massive marble statue of Achilles came crashing down on top of him.

CHAPTER 3

Marcus dove to the ground, his chin smacking the hard stone. He braced himself for the crushing blow of thousands of pounds of marble hitting him. He heard a terrible *crash*!

But he felt nothing.

He peeled open his eyes and peered around.

To his amazement, the broken statue was just behind him. It must have sailed right over him. Marcus whispered a thank-you to the gods.

Poor Achilles had lost his head, which was now rolling slowly in the street.

Marcus could practically hear the warrior's deathly cries.

But Marcus himself was in one piece, and the earth had stopped shaking.

Marcus pulled himself up. He put his hand to his chin, and it came away streaked with blood. Otherwise he was unhurt.

A humpbacked street vendor came up to him. "Don't even think about stealing those apples," he barked, reaching down and snatching two apples that had escaped from his baskets.

"I wouldn't," Marcus said, spotting a third hidden behind the fountain. He should give it to the man, he knew. But just the thought of the juicy apple made his stomach flip with joy. Festus fed his slaves nothing but watery gruel and old cheese. The fruit seller didn't spot it, and Marcus said nothing.

"That giant beast must be restless," said the man, spitting on one of the apples and rubbing it against his rough tunic.

"Giant?" Marcus asked.

"Everyone knows that's why the earth is shaking," the man replied, looking at Marcus as though he must be stupid not to know this. "There's a great beast living under the mountain. Every few years it wakes up and the city shakes. Then it goes to sleep again."

Marcus thought of his father — Tata. Talk of monsters and magic always made Tata shake his head. Tata said it was only natural that people would make up stories or blame the gods for what they couldn't understand — wild storms and killing fevers, dead crops and mad dogs. But science always held the answer, Tata believed, if you looked hard enough.

Marcus didn't say this now. It wasn't right for a slave to correct the opinion of a free man, even if the man was just a poor fruit seller.

What amazed Marcus was that people in Pompeii just accepted these tremors, shrugging them off as they would a rainstorm. Even now, shoppers were already back to haggling for bargains.

The fruit seller turned away and Marcus

grabbed the hidden apple, slipping it into his pocket. He picked up the heavy laundry sack and threw it onto his back with a sigh. Festus wouldn't care if a monster really had come stomping through Pompeii. Marcus had better get back to his master's villa soon, or he'd be greeted with a beating.

He was turning to leave when he noticed an old woman sitting in the street, dazed. The shaking must have knocked her down. Passersby stepped around her as if she were a heap of trash. Marcus ignored the woman; there were beggars everywhere, after all.

But she looked so miserable.

With a sigh, he once again dropped the laundry sack. He went to the woman, crouching down next to her. She was a beggar, it seemed, her tunic stained and tattered, her bare feet crusted with sores.

She scowled at him. "Scat, thief!"

"I wasn't going to steal anything," Marcus said. He should have ignored the hag like everyone else did.

But then the woman's face softened. She studied Marcus with her catlike green eyes. She was very old, with sagging cheeks and deep wrinkles. But Marcus could imagine that a long time ago she might have been pretty.

"What do you want, then?" she asked.

Almost without thinking, he reached into his pocket and took out the apple. "Here," he said. She looked hungrier than he was.

The woman took the apple in one of her gnarled hands. "Help me up, please."

Marcus held her arms as she got to her feet, and stood with her as she steadied herself. And then she suddenly grabbed his hand, gripping it with surprising strength.

"Be careful, kind boy," she whispered. "I have seen the signs. Terrible doom is coming for the people of Pompeii."

She leaned so close that he smelled the strange spices on her breath.

"When hope is lost, *follow the hand of Mercury.*" She stepped back. "Do you understand?"

Marcus had no idea what she meant. All over Pompeii there were statues of the powerful messenger god, with his winged sandals and helmet. But what did that matter to him?

"I understand," he lied. Now he just wanted to get away from her.

"The end is coming," she said, finally letting go of his hand. "This world will burn!"

CHAPTER 4

Marcus had barely blinked and the woman was gone, swallowed by the crowd.

He felt a stab of fear as he thought of what she had said.

Was she a witch who could predict the future? A priestess who could hear the whispers of the gods?

Marcus thought again of his father. Tata would know what was happening here.

A wave of sadness crashed over him. If only Tata were with him now!

He could picture his father so clearly — his gentle blue eyes glinting through a mop of golden hair.

Tata was born in Germania, a kingdom just beyond the northern boundaries of this vast Roman Empire. When Tata was just ten years old, Roman soldiers had invaded his village. Marcus's father was soon captured, sold to slave traders, and marched hundreds of miles in chains to the empire's capital city of Rome.

But Tata was lucky. He was bought by a kind man, a writer and scientist named Linus Selius. He taught Tata to read and write in Latin, the language of the empire. He took Tata on research trips to faraway lands, teaching him all he knew about the natural world. Soon, Tata was helping Linus research his books and coming up with theories of his own.

The years passed. Tata married Marcus's mother, who died when Marcus was just a baby. Marcus grew up helping Tata in Linus's library, one of the finest in Rome.

Tata was always trying to get Marcus interested in studying nature, reading him his latest theories and dragging him on long walks through the hills above Rome.

But it was the ancient Greek stories written centuries before that Marcus loved most, especially the tales of the great heroes like Odysseus and Hercules.

How Marcus had loved his happy life with Tata!

But then, two months ago, Linus Selius had died in a fever that swept through Rome. In a blink, Marcus's entire world crumbled. Marcus and Tata became the property of Linus's nephew, the brutal Festus Julius. Linus himself had always despised Festus, and the nephew wasted no time destroying his uncle's happy home. Within two days, Tata was sold. Marcus was loaded onto a donkey cart and brought here to Pompeii, a two-day trip from Rome. He was now one of ten slaves working endless days in Festus's enormous villa, one of the grandest homes in Pompeii.

Where was Tata? He could be anywhere in the vast Roman Empire by now, from the rocky cliffs of Britannia to the deserts of Africa.

His thoughts carried Marcus far away, until a blaring trumpet yanked him back.

"It's the gladiator parade!" an old man cried out with excitement. "It's the fighters who will appear tomorrow!"

People jammed the sidewalks, so Marcus could not get through. Now he had no choice but to put down the laundry sack and wait.

Two men on white horses led the parade, their riders waving bright flags. A band of horn players followed, and then acrobats and jugglers, and finally, a stout man with a leering smile. He was the *lanista* — the owner of these gladiators.

The lanista waved at the crowd, proud as an emperor. Owning gladiators was a dirty business; no respectable person would do it. But the lanista had grown rich on the blood of his gladiators, and he held his head high.

And then there was Cyclops, led by two young women in bright robes who were throwing rose petals.

"There he is!" a woman in the crowd shrieked, pointing at the muscled brute.

The champion wore a gleaming bronze helmet. His massive shield matched the armor strapped to his bulging legs and arms. A leather patch hid his blind eye. Scars covered his face. Marcus had heard terrifying stories about this man — that he had jaws like a tiger's, that his battle cry was like a panther's scream, that he could snap a man's neck with one hand.

The crowd cheered and hooted as Cyclops passed.

But people stood silently as the next four men walked by. These were the wretched souls who would be thrown into the arena with Cyclops tomorrow. None of them had a chance against Cyclops. By tomorrow afternoon, they'd all be dead.

Marcus couldn't bear to watch them. But then he caught sight of the last man in line.

Marcus froze, staring.

The man was tall, with golden hair streaming out of his bronze helmet. He walked slowly, with dignity. A guard followed him, jabbing him in the back with a spear to move him along.

The man turned his head, and the sun lit up his proud face and glinting blue eyes.

Could it be?

The pounding in Marcus's heart told the answer.

And suddenly Marcus was running wildly into the street.

"Tata!" Marcus screamed.

CHAPTER 5

Tata froze and looked up, searching the crowd frantically with his eyes.

The guard screamed at him, "Move! Move now!"

At last Tata spotted Marcus. He dropped his shield and ran toward him. Seconds later, Marcus was in Tata's arms.

"It's not possible!" Tata whispered, hugging him so tightly that Marcus could hardly breathe. "How did you get here?"

"Festus brought me here after you were sold,"

Marcus said, barely able to choke out the words. "But Tata! How . . . why . . ."

Not even in Marcus's nightmares could he have imagined anything worse than this: Festus had sold Tata to the gladiators.

Marcus buried his face in Tata's chest, breathing in his familiar smell. Every day — every hour — Marcus had wished for this moment. And for a few seconds he let himself believe that they were really back together, that his prayers had been answered.

But, of course, the opposite was true.

Two guards grabbed Tata's arms, tearing him away from Marcus.

And then the lanista appeared.

"What's this!" he spat. "How dare you stop my parade!"

The musicians were silent, the jugglers and acrobats still. All eyes were on Tata and Marcus.

"Have mercy!" Tata said, struggling in the guards' grip. "This is my son!"

The lanista stared at Marcus, his cold, fishy eyes looking him up and down.

"Maybe you'd like to join your father in the arena?" he sneered.

Then the lanista looked to the crowd. "What do you think?" he bellowed. "A father and son against Cyclops!"

A few people shouted.

"Bring him!"

"Yes!"

"What a show it will be!"

"Or maybe you should fight each other?" the lanista said, rubbing his hands together.

"Run from here, Marcus!" his father cried. "Go!"

But instead, Marcus grabbed the lanista's arm. "I beg you! Please let my father go!"

The man ripped his arm away and snatched a spear from one of the guards. He pointed the blade at Marcus's eye. "Ever wondered how Cyclops lost his eye?" he taunted, lunging at Marcus.

"No!" Tata shouted.

Marcus staggered back. He lost his balance and fell, smacking his head on the stone curb. His head exploded in pain. He struggled to sit up, and through the blur he could see Tata being dragged away, the guards jabbing him with spears. The lanista's wicked cackle rose up over the merry music.

As Tata disappeared, all of the strength drained from Marcus's body. These past two months, he'd always had the hope that he and Tata would be together again. And that speck of hope — a tiny glowing ember — had been everything to him.

But now . . .

Marcus lay back in the gutter, closing his eyes.

How would he go on?

In his mind he pictured Festus's face, heard his barking orders. He imagined the slaves who'd been working in the villa for years. Their bodies were crooked and scarred, their eyes dead like statues'.

And then Marcus thought of the heroes from his favorite stories. They had desperate moments, too: Odysseus, who was lost at sea for ten years on his way home from Troy. Hercules, pinned down by a bloodthirsty lion.

Those courageous men knew terror and hopelessness, as Marcus did now.

But their stories hadn't ended with fear and defeat.

Marcus's eyes snapped open. He sat up and struggled to his feet.

He understood.

He would try to save Tata, even if it killed him.

CHAPTER 6

Marcus went to the fountain and splashed cool water on his face.

He didn't have much time. Soon the parade would reach the gladiator barracks, and Tata would be locked away. The barracks was like a prison, with high stone walls and a towering iron gate. Marcus had heard that the fighters were locked in dark cells, their arms and legs shackled, until it was time to fight.

Once Tata was in the barracks, it would be too late.

Somehow, Marcus had to steal Tata away from the parade.

But how?

He searched his mind for ideas. Again, he thought of Odysseus.

Odysseus wasn't the strongest man. But he was cunning. There had come a low point in the Trojan War when the Greek armies had Troy surrounded, but they could not break through the massive wall that encircled the city. Thousands of Trojan archers guarded the wall, ready to fire down on anyone who came close. Some Greek generals were ready to give up on invading the city of Troy.

Not Odysseus.

He came up with the ingenious idea of building a giant wooden horse with a hollow belly. He and his best Greek soldiers hid inside the horse. They made the Trojans believe the wooden animal was an offering from the gods, and tricked them into bringing it inside their walls.

And then — *attack!*

In the dead of night, Odysseus and the hidden soldiers snuck out of the horse and opened the gates. The Greek soldiers smashed the Trojan army and conquered the city.

Marcus searched around. All he saw was the laundry bag, lying where he had dropped it.

But wait . . .

The idea flashed into Marcus's mind, and before he could talk himself out of it, he had ripped the sack open and was rummaging through Festus's clothes.

He grabbed a toga, a robe woven from the finest wool and edged with purple ribbon. Marcus couldn't build himself a wooden horse. But he could hide in Festus's toga, disguise himself as an important Roman citizen.

Marcus threw it around himself, covering his old tunic. The toga stank like rotten food, old wine, and Festus's sweat. Marcus fought back his nausea as he wrapped the endless stretch of fabric around his body, finally draping the loose end over his shoulder.

He straightened his shoulders. The toga dragged on the ground a bit, but it would do. Marcus spat into his hands and flattened his hair to his forehead, the style of a rich son of Rome.

Now he just needed a weapon, something to scare the guards so he and Tata could escape.

Once again, the answer was right in front of him, on the sidewalk: the snake charmer.

Somehow, the old man was still dozing with the basket at his feet.

Marcus crept up, kneeled, and snatched the basket.

The old man was awake in a flash, hollering after him. "Stop him! Stop that thief!"

Marcus darted through the crowd, one hand firmly on the lid of the basket. He was terrified that the lid would fly off, that the cobra would spring out and sink its fangs into Marcus's neck. He could feel the snake hissing ferociously, banging its body against the sides of the flimsy basket.

Marcus's heart pounded, his legs wobbled, his mind swirled with fear. But somehow he kept himself moving until he caught up with the parade.

The music had stopped and the lanista was unlocking the gates of the gladiator barracks.

Marcus was almost out of time.

And he would have just one chance.

CHAPTER 7

Marcus stepped slowly, clutching the basket. At first he didn't notice how people moved aside for him, how slaves bowed their heads. And then he understood: His disguise was working! Nobody guessed he was just a slave.

None of the guards tried to stop him as he approached the front of the parade. Marcus saw the lanista, his chest puffed out. And there was Tata. The big guard was jabbing him in the back with a spear, laughing at Tata's pain.

Marcus's blood boiled as he walked toward the lanista.

Closer . . .

Closer . . .

Closer . . .

When he was just a few feet away, the lanista looked at him. Their eyes met, and Marcus saw the flash of recognition in the man's eyes.

"Stop him!" the lanista bellowed, pointing to Marcus.

But it was too late. Marcus tore the lid off the basket. He lunged forward. And with all the strength he could gather, he thrust the open basket toward the lanista, propelling the snake into the air.

The cobra soared, a twisting, hissing arrow. The snake struck the lanista in the chest and then landed on the ground, coiling itself tightly.

The lanista's womanly scream rose up over the crowd.

And everything went still and silent.

People stared, hypnotized by the sight of the cobra.

The creature lifted its head, rising, rising, rising, until it was as tall as a child. It flared its great hood and then opened its mouth to expose its silky pink mouth and killer fangs.

Hisssssssssssssssssssssssssssssssss!

And then, as if Marcus himself had pulled a lever, the earth started to rumble, just as it had earlier. Stones crumbled and fell from the wall surrounding the barracks. A roar echoed from deep under the ground.

"It's a curse from the gods!" someone shouted.

The crowd erupted in panic.

The lanista turned and ran, and his guards followed.

Gladiators bolted. The snake slithered away.

The horses screeched and reared up, tossing their riders to the ground.

Marcus ran to Tata, who stared at him in confusion.

"Tata!" Marcus said, tossing off his toga. "It's me!"

Amazement lit up Tata's eyes, but there was not a second to spare.

Tata grabbed Marcus's hand as though he would never let it go.

"This way!" Tata said, pulling Marcus to one of the riderless horses. It was a ragged white mare that looked a hundred years old. One of her ears looked as if it had been chewed off. Tata grabbed the reins and soothed the horse while Marcus climbed on. Tata climbed on in front of Marcus. "Hold on tight," he said, snapping the reins.

Marcus doubted the old horse could even run. But she shot forward and was soon speeding them down the street.

Marcus clung to Tata, his heart pounding in terror. He expected spears to fly after them, a dagger to stab him in the middle of his back. But the horse ran faster and faster; it seemed she was as eager to escape her life in Pompeii as they were.

They moved so fast that Marcus felt as though they were flying. Closing his eyes, he imagined that this old white mare was the winged horse Pegasus, and that they were soaring through the clouds.

When he opened his eyes, he was shocked to see they had passed through the city gates.

Tata raised his fist to the heavens and let out a Latin cheer.

"Ecce!"

They had made it.

CHAPTER 8

THAT AFTERNOON
THE ROAD TO VESUVIUS

They headed for the mountain Vesuvius, a massive triangle of green that loomed up to the east of Pompeii. As they left the city behind, Tata ripped the armor from his shoulders and legs, and threw the pieces into a ditch. He left his helmet in a field of wheat, a trade for the old tunic he snatched from the farmer's drying line.

They rode for hours, crossing orchards and olive groves, pastures and fields.

Night was coming, and Tata decided they should stop in a patch of woods halfway up the mountain.

They got off the mare and stretched their aching legs.

Marcus reached into his pocket and pulled out a handful of grapes he'd snatched from a vineyard they'd passed through.

"Hungry, Peg?" Marcus said to the mare.

"Peg?" Tata asked, arching one of his bushy brows.

"Short for Pegasus," Marcus said.

Tata smiled, stroking the mare's nose.

Marcus fed the grapes to Peg one by one, until they were all gone.

Peg smacked her lips and rubbed Marcus's cheek with her nose.

"We have a friend for life, it seems," Tata said.

Peg nickered as though she agreed, and Marcus and Tata laughed.

It was that moment, as their laughter filled the air, that it really hit Marcus: This was not a dream, not a wish, not a desperate prayer to the gods.

He and Tata were together! A jolt of happiness practically lifted him off the ground. And Tata seemed to feel it, too. They looked at each other and smiled.

But then a shadow passed over Marcus's heart. Because as happy as he felt at this moment, he knew they were in terrible danger.

"They'll come after us," Marcus whispered.

The slave hunters. Festus would hire the best, most cunning men, experts in tracking their prey.

"They won't look for us up here," Tata promised. "The hunters will be searching Pompeii. It will be days before they come to the mountain. And by then we'll be gone. We'll head back to Rome, Marcus. I have no doubt that Linus's friends will help us. Somehow I need to continue Linus's work."

It amazed Marcus that Tata could be so certain, so filled with hope. He draped an arm around

Marcus's shoulders and looked up into the sky, admiring the bright moon and the swirl of stars.

But what Marcus saw in the bright moonlight was the angry bruise on Tata's cheek, the purple scar zigzagging along his chin. How Tata must have suffered these past two months!

Marcus had already told Tata about his time with Festus. The words had poured out of him during their ride up the mountain, until at last he had told Tata about every last moment of his time with his brutal master.

But Tata hadn't said a thing about being with the gladiators.

And now Marcus wanted to know.

"Will you tell me what happened to you, Tata?" Marcus said.

Pain flashed through Tata's eyes and he looked away from Marcus.

"That is the past now," he said.

And from his tone, Marcus knew that he must not ask again.

But he couldn't help thinking about what his father must have been through. And it made his blood boil.

"I hate that lanista!" Marcus burst out. "And I hate Festus! I hate all of them for what they did to you, Tata! We need to get even!"

Yes, Marcus thought, they'd get revenge! They'd set fire to Festus's villa! Find the lanista and . . .

But Tata whipped around, gripping Marcus's shoulders.

"No, Marcus," he snapped. "Never speak like

that. You must never let hatred take over! Then you are no better than Festus! And hatred like that will destroy you."

Marcus blinked, stung by Tata's sharp tone.

"I'm sorry, Tata," Marcus said.

Tata's face softened. "There is goodness in the world, Marcus, and kindness. You cannot forget that."

Goodness? Kindness?

Marcus had seen none of that lately.

If there was one thing Marcus had learned these past two months, it was this: The world was a dark, evil place. Only the most ruthless would survive.

But Marcus said none of that to Tata, who would not approve of such dark thoughts.

And they were both so tired. They led Peg into a small grove of trees and tied her up for the night.

Tata stretched out on a grassy patch.

"Tomorrow our new life begins," he whispered, and within seconds he was fast asleep.

Marcus lay down next to Tata, but he couldn't get comfortable. His muscles ached from the long ride. But it was the strange noises that kept snapping him awake — distant rumbles, low hisses. Was he dreaming? Once, he drifted to sleep, but was awakened when the earth seemed to be shaking. He sat up, wondering if Tata felt it, too.

But Tata was sound asleep.

Was Marcus imagining things? Maybe what he was hearing were just the rumbles of his own angry heart.

But Peg seemed restless, too, stamping her feet, snorting.

Finally Marcus got up and stood with her, stroking her patchy fur, resting his cheek against her warm head. He looked down at Pompeii, dimly lit by oil lamps and torches. He made out the shapes of the houses crowded together along the city walls, the boats moored in the harbor.

Marcus hugged Peg.

"It's okay," he told her. "We're with Tata now. We're safe up here."

He knew that was true, that the slave hunters were far away, that Festus was too busy with his important guests to be thinking too much about his escaped slave.

Still, Marcus couldn't shake the feeling that there was something lurking up here on the mountain, something even more dangerous than the slave hunters.

But what could it be?

CHAPTER 9

It was close to dawn when Marcus finally fell asleep.

And right away, he tumbled into a dream.

He was on a quest with Hercules to kill the monstrous Hydra, an enormous serpent with nine heads. Just one puff of her poisonous breath could kill.

Marcus waded silently through the dark and misty swamp, pushing aside sharp stalks of grass. And then, just ahead, there she was: the hideous serpent. Marcus stopped, frozen, as the beast rose

up from the swamp. One by one, her nine horrific heads emerged from the mist, staring at him with glowing yellow eyes, leering with dripping, glistening fangs.

And then —

Huff.

A burning, rotten stench rushed into Marcus's lungs.

The poisonous Hydra breath!

Marcus gagged and coughed.

His throat burned. His chest felt as if it would explode!

"Marcus! Marcus!" a voice called.

Hercules?

"Marcus!"

Marcus's eyes popped open, and the nightmare fell away. Tata was kneeling next to him, calling his name, shaking him awake.

It was all a dream!

Relief poured over him as he realized he wasn't in a swamp with the Hydra. He was on the mountain Vesuvius, with Tata.

But wait . . . something was terribly wrong.

The air was still poisonous! The Hydra was still puffing gusts of her burning breath into Marcus's lungs.

But there was no Hydra.

That burning, poisonous smell was *here*.

"Marcus," Tata choked. "Get up! The air has gone bad!"

Tata helped pull Marcus to his feet and they staggered together toward Peg.

Marcus's head pounded. Tears poured from his stinging eyes. His lungs were on fire and he gasped for breath. He felt dizzy. They couldn't last much longer in this air!

Peg was rearing in panic, white foam spewing from her mouth.

Tata fumbled with her rope, finally untying it.

They all stumbled out of the grove of trees, where the air was miraculously clear.

Tata and Marcus collapsed to the ground, gulping the fresh air into their lungs.

"Tata," Marcus rasped. "What was that?"

"Sulfur gas," Tata replied, his voice ragged from coughing. "There's no doubt. I smelled it once before, when Linus and I were visiting a gold mine in Africa. We were deep underground. Sulfur gas can be deadly. It can kill in minutes. We barely made it to the surface in time."

Tata looked back into the grove of trees. "It's highly unusual to find sulfur gas above the ground," he said.

He stood and climbed onto a boulder that

jutted out from the grassy slope, looking all around. Marcus saw a hint of worry in his father's eyes. But mainly what he saw was curiosity, a hunger to learn and understand. It was the same look Tata used to get in Linus Selius's library when he was chasing down a new theory. Suddenly, Tata was not a slave on the run. He was a scientist, searching for answers.

And the truth was that after spending a lifetime working with Linus, Tata probably knew more about science and nature than most people in the empire. In recent years, Linus would ask Tata to join him when important guests came, eager for his friends to hear Tata's ideas.

Tata hopped down from the boulder.

He held out his hand to Marcus, pulling him to his feet.

"Let's keep heading up the mountain," he said, handing Marcus Peg's reins. "We'll discover more as we get closer to the top."

Tata set out, climbing the rocky path.

Marcus took a deep breath, and gave Peg's reins a tug.

But the mare didn't budge.

She looked at Marcus with her wise brown eyes. Her expression was so thoughtful. Marcus would not have been shocked if she had opened her mouth and started to speak to him.

"What is it?" Marcus said.

The mare looked up the mountain.

She stamped her foot.

"You don't want to go up there, do you?"

Snort.

"Me neither," Marcus said.

Tata's voice shouted out. "Marcus!"

Marcus and Peg eyed each other.

"We can't let Tata head up there by himself," Marcus said.

Peg made a noise that sounded like a sigh, and she stepped forward.

Together they followed Tata toward the top of Vesuvius.

CHAPTER 10

AUGUST 24

7:00 A.M.

THE MOUNTAIN VESUVIUS

They took the twisting path that wound up the mountain.

The sun was barely up, but already it roasted their backs.

Tata kept stopping to look around. He seemed to be taking the mountain apart with his eyes, inch by inch. He kept crouching down, scooping

162

up handfuls of soil, rubbing it between his fingers. He ripped up pieces of grass, sniffing them, and even touching them to his tongue.

"Do you notice the quiet?" he asked at one point. "There are no birds or insects anywhere."

Tata was right.

Normally at this time of morning, the air would be alive with chirping and singing and chattering. But Marcus had not seen one creature since they came up on the mountain, not a deer, a squirrel, nor even a fly. No people, either. There were pastures on this side of Vesuvius, and they'd passed two shepherd shacks. But they hadn't seen a soul.

"Where did they all go?" Marcus asked, trying to keep his voice from shaking.

"It might be that there's not enough water," Tata said. "It could be the heat drove them off."

They'd already discovered that the streams higher up on the mountain were mysteriously dried up. They'd managed to find just one that still ran. And the trickle of water tasted so foul they could barely choke it down. Peg wouldn't go near it, even though she'd barely had a drink since before they'd slept last night. Maybe that was why she was walking so slowly, why she kept stopping and stamping her feet.

But now, as they passed through a cluster of pine trees, Peg stopped short. Tata pulled at her rope, but she refused to move. Marcus gave her a pat.

"Come on, Peg," he said.

The mare refused to budge.

She looked at Marcus with wide, fearful eyes.

Neigh!

Was she trying to warn them about something?

Marcus found the answer when he peered through the trees, into a meadow. The first thing he noticed was the grass was brown, as though it had been burned.

Then he saw the sheep — at least twenty of them — all splayed out on their sides or backs.

Marcus knew right away that they were all dead.

"Good Jupiter," Tata whispered in shock, stepping slowly into the field.

Once again, Marcus had to force himself to follow his father.

Tata crouched down next to one of the sheep.

"There's not a mark on her," Tata said, laying a gentle hand over the poor creature's head.

It was true — there was not a speck of blood, no bite marks, no wounds at all.

But her tongue bulged out of her mouth and her eyes were wide in agony.

All the sheep looked the same.

What could have killed them?

Tata said a prayer in his old Germanic language and then stood up.

"I've seen enough," he said. "We must leave here. Now."

But as they turned, there was a low rumbling from deep inside the earth. It quickly rose to a roar as the ground started to shake. Marcus half expected a great beast to burst through the soil, for a giant clawed hand to grab him around the throat.

What he saw next was almost more horrifying.

As the ground boiled, the field suddenly ripped apart right in front of them. The gaping crack looked like an evil smiling mouth, ready to devour them. Great chunks of earth and dead sheep tumbled into the blackness. Marcus and Tata staggered back.

And then —

Boom!

An explosion shattered the air. Fire leaped out of the crack, a massive flaming tongue that seemed to lick the sky and then disappear.

The force of the blast knocked them over, and sent Marcus tumbling down the steep slope.

He rolled and twisted, his neck cracking, his arms tangling, his face scraping the rocky dirt as he slid down the hill.

He crashed into a tree, which knocked every bit of air out of his lungs.

Finally the ground stopped shaking. The fire was gone. But now ash rained down on them, a silent blizzard of hot flakes.

Marcus sat there, numb with terror, dizzy from his fall.

Tata came hurtling down the hill with Peg.

"Are you hurt?" he gasped, dropping to his knees next to Marcus.

Marcus shook his head dumbly, slowly rising to his feet.

Moments later, they were speeding down the mountain on Peg.

The mare ran like she had the day before, her hooves barely touching the ground.

Finally, Tata spoke.

"A terrible fire is burning under the mountain," he warned. "I believe the entire mountain will explode."

Marcus was too stunned to speak, or even think.

All he could hear was a ragged voice whispering in his mind.

The beggar woman's voice.

"This world will burn."

CHAPTER 11

Tata was silent for most of the ride down, hunkered deep inside his thoughts. Marcus could sense that he was trying to assemble a huge puzzle in his mind, to make sense out of all they had seen.

As they came to the bottom of the mountain, Tata had his theory, and he explained it all to Marcus in terrifying detail.

"Some mountains are not just solid rock," Tata began. "They are filled with gases and fire and melted rock. Virgil wrote about such a mountain in Greece, called Etna."

Virgil was one of Rome's most famous writers.

"Virgil told of a terrible eruption, maybe a hundred years ago," Tata continued. "He said that fire and ash shot from the mountain into the sky, that day turned to night, and a burning cloud swept down the mountain, destroying everything in its path."

Tata turned to look at Marcus.

"I never imagined it could be true," Tata said. "I thought it was just an exciting tale. But now we've seen for ourselves."

Yes, they had, though Marcus still couldn't quite believe it had all happened. The earth tremors. Killer clouds. Foul water. Dead sheep. Flames shooting out of the ground. And that terrifying explosion. It was stranger than any tale Marcus had ever read.

"It all makes sense," Tata said. "What is happening now on Vesuvius tells me that the worst is yet to come, that the entire mountain is about to explode."

Marcus shivered, though the heat was searing.

"Will Pompeii be destroyed?" he said.

Tata was silent for a moment.

"I have no doubt," Tata said finally.

Marcus held Tata tighter.

"I met an old woman yesterday, a beggar," he said, remembering the woman's shining green eyes and gnarled hands. "She said the strangest things to me — that Pompeii was doomed, that the city would burn. I thought she was a madwoman. But what she said was right! She could read the future!"

"I don't believe in prophets and witches," Tata said. "But nature sends out warnings. Why do you think all of the animals have fled? They felt the tremors, scented the sulfur, tasted the water. Their instincts told them to flee. Linus would say that the old woman is keenly sensitive — or that she has the mind of a great scientist."

It was hard to imagine that poor old hag discussing science with Tata and Linus. But what Tata said made sense.

"Where will we go?" Marcus asked.

Tata didn't answer right away.

Then he slowed Peg to a stop and turned in the saddle to face Marcus.

"We need to warn the people of Pompeii," he said. "They have no idea what is about to happen. If we don't warn them, they could all be killed."

It took Marcus a moment for Tata's words to sink in.

Was he really saying they should go to the very city about to be destroyed? A city where slave hunters were prowling through every alley with their spears and chains?

Marcus didn't want to go anywhere near that wretched city! He and Tata needed to save themselves, to get as far away as they could. Now!

"I don't understand," Marcus said.

Tata touched Marcus's hand. "But you do. There are more than ten thousand people living in Pompeii. It's our duty to warn them of what is about to happen."

Marcus tried to look away from Tata, but their eyes were locked together.

And Marcus recognized something in Tata's gaze.

It was the same determined look that Marcus had always imagined on the faces of his heroes as they prepared for their battles.

Hadn't Odysseus and Hercules risked their lives over and over? Hadn't they plunged into danger without thinking about whether they'd come out alive?

Marcus had read so many stories of heroic warriors. But it was only now, looking at his father, that he finally understood what it meant to have honor, to be a hero.

Marcus reached deep inside himself, trying to summon some courage of his own.

To his surprise, he found more than he expected.

He sat taller. "Yes, I understand, Tata."

Marcus saw the flash of pride on Tata's face before he turned back around. He gave Peg a pat.

And off they galloped, on their tattered mare, toward the doomed city of Pompeii.

CHAPTER 12

The sun was high in the sky as they approached the city.

They tied Peg to a tree in an olive grove, about a half mile from Pompeii's eastern gates.

Marcus hugged Peg. "I'll be back."

The mare nosed him in the chest, looking him in the eye.

The ground rumbled again — the tremors were definitely getting stronger.

Marcus looked back nervously at the mountain and loosened Peg's rope.

"If we're not back, you need to break free from here and get out on your own."

Peg eyed him.

"You understand me?" he said. "Don't wait for us."

The mare snorted.

Marcus hoped that meant yes.

He hugged her one last time, and Tata rubbed her nose before they headed for the city gates.

Tata's plan was to speak to Pompeii's magistrates — the men elected to lead the city. They would know the best way to warn the people of Pompeii.

Marcus and Tata wove through the crowded streets, keeping their eyes out for men who might help — and those who might be hunting for them.

It didn't take long to reach the Forum — an open square surrounded by five buildings and the city's main temple, dedicated to Jupiter. Statues of emperors and generals seemed to glare at Marcus as he followed Tata to the magistrates' building. Marcus's heart pounded as they approached the entrance, where three steely-looking guards stood watch.

"Stop, slave," a guard ordered.

Tata held his head up.

"Sir, I have an urgent message for the city's leaders. The city is in danger. We must warn the people of Pompeii."

The man barely glanced at Tata from beneath his helmet.

"Be gone," the guard ordered, shooing him as though he were a stray dog.

"Sir," Tata said. "It's the mountain. There will soon be a terrible explosion. We —"

The guard raised his spear menacingly.

"Go from here! Nobody in there wants to talk to a filthy slave!"

Suddenly Marcus couldn't help but see what the guard saw when he looked at Tata. With his tattered tunic and body stained with bruises, Tata looked little better than the beggar woman.

The other guards stepped up, their spears glinting in the sun.

This was hopeless, Marcus realized.

"You are making a mistake," Tata warned, taking Marcus's arm and hurrying him away.

They walked out of the Forum and headed toward the main street.

"We'll have to tell people ourselves," Tata said. "We'll go to the shops and restaurants. Hopefully some people will listen."

Marcus hoped Tata couldn't read his thoughts: They were wasting their time. Nobody would take the word of a slave.

They stood on the sidewalk, waiting to cross the crowded street.

Two laughing little boys ran behind their mother. One held a wooden sword.

"I'm Cyclops!" the boy sang.

The gladiator match! That's where everyone was heading!

Marcus watched the boys, but then his eyes drifted up to Vesuvius.

What he saw stopped his heart: a wisp of smoke, rising out of the peak.

The mountain seemed to be coming alive.

"Tata . . ." Marcus pointed up at the smoking mountain.

Tata stared in horror — and fascination.

They both stood there, their eyes glued to the mountain. Which is why they didn't see the golden chariot that had stopped suddenly right in front of them — or the pair of cold, pale eyes that glared at them.

By the time Marcus saw Festus and his guards rushing toward them, it was too late. Penned in by the crowds, he and Tata were trapped.

And seconds later Marcus was staring at the glinting tip of a spear.

"Idiots," Festus hissed. "You actually believed you could escape?"

Tata shook his arm from the guard's grip and stepped toward Festus.

"Sir, please, a disaster is coming. The mountain is about to explode. People must leave the city right away."

Festus laughed cruelly. "You think you can save yourself by telling tales?"

The guard grabbed Tata roughly, and once again Tata shook himself free. He seemed to be gaining strength from the crowd, from the fear and panic in the eyes of the people all around them.

"You've felt the earth tremors. And now look

at the mountain. You can see for yourself, the smoke! Any moment it's going to explode."

Festus didn't even look at the mountain. He put his face close to Tata's, screaming, "You dare try to outsmart me? You think I'm a fool?"

"Think of your uncle, sir, of Linus," Tata said, struggling as the guard gripped him again. "He would agree with me. I'm certain."

Festus's fat cheeks turned bright red.

"My uncle was a weak-minded idiot," Festus said, spitting out the words. "He cared more for a slave than me, a man who shared his own blood!"

And suddenly it was all clear to Marcus — why Festus had sold Tata so quickly.

Few people in Rome were as admired as Linus Selius. And yet he had never been impressed by Festus's chariots and villas and fine stallions. Linus knew the truth about his nephew, that he made his money by cheating people.

Tata had the one thing that Festus's fortune couldn't buy: his uncle's respect.

And Festus hated Tata for it. He hated him so much that he would make Tata suffer the worst fate imaginable: death in the arena.

"Take this slave to the lanista!" Festus ordered. "He will be just in time for his match against Cyclops."

As the guards dragged his father away, Marcus's blood boiled in his veins. His heart smoldered with hatred.

He stepped close to Festus, looking him squarely in his fishlike eyes.

"You are evil."

"Marcus!" Tata gasped.

Marcus couldn't miss the flicker of shock on Festus's face.

But, of course, Festus had the last word.

"Take the boy to the lanista, too. Tell him it's a gift from me. It will be quite a show today for the people of Pompeii."

As the guards took hold of Marcus, something exploded deep inside him.

He opened his mouth to scream, to curse Festus and this dark and evil world.

But it was not Marcus's voice that filled the air.

It was the voice of Vesuvius — two shattering explosions.

BOOM!

BOOM!

CHAPTER 13

The ground shook as Marcus had never felt before, as though hundreds of monsters were waking up in their underground caves, pounding the earth in fits of fury.

Panicking, the guards let go of Marcus and Tata. Marcus ran to his father and clung to him, struggling to stay upright as the earth rose and fell like waves on a wild river.

The top of the mountain had blown off, and from the jagged opening gushed an enormous billowing brown cloud. The cloud seemed to stretch into the heavens. Flames shot through the smoke as jagged bolts of lightning ripped at the sky.

People streamed out of the shops. Beggars rose to their feet. Slaves dropped their bundles of wood and water jugs.

For a moment, nobody spoke. Nobody even seemed to be breathing.

All eyes were on the mountain.

But then came the shouts.

"It's the end of the world!"

"Why are the gods punishing us?"

"Everyone must leave Pompeii!" Tata shouted. He started pulling Marcus through the crowd.

But Festus called to his guards. "No! Stop those slaves!" Festus bellowed.

The guards lunged for Marcus and Tata.

But Tata held up his hand. "You must listen!" he boomed. Somehow his voice rose up over the roar of Vesuvius.

To Marcus's shock, the guards did not move. They were just as scared as everyone else.

"If you want to live, you must leave now," Tata warned. He spoke not only to the guards but to the gathering crowd. "Get out of the city, and go as far away from the mountain as you can."

Just then a man stepped out of Festus's chariot. His fine toga swished around his powerful body. In his hand flashed the seal of a senator, one of the most powerful men in Pompeii. But it was not Festus that this man had come out to talk to. It was Tata.

"What you say about the mountain," he demanded. "How do you know this?"

Festus stepped up. "He is just —"

The man silenced Festus with a wave of his hand.

"Speak," he ordered Tata.

Tata did not shrink back from the powerful man. He met his challenging gaze.

"Sir, for years my master was the scientist Linus Selius. My son and I were on the mountain last night. We saw many signs that this disaster was coming. Soon it will be too late to escape with our lives."

The man looked up on the mountain, at the boiling ash cloud that now filled the sky. The mountain's power seemed to be growing. It was now only a matter of time before this blanket of doom fell over the city.

"How much time do we have?"

"A few hours at the most," Tata said. "The worst will come after the mountain runs out of power. I believe all of the gases and ash in the sky will come back down, and explode. A great wave of fire will sweep down over Pompeii."

"Dear gods," the man whispered. A mask seemed to drop from his face, baring his fear. "Festus," he said. "We must warn the magistrates at once! We must order people to leave the city!"

And before Festus could reply, the man had rushed off. With surprising speed, he sprinted across the Forum. He rushed past the guards and disappeared into the government building.

"This is nonsense —" Festus bellowed.

But his words were cut off by a loud *whoosh* from the sky just above them.

Marcus looked up just in time to see a giant flaming fireball closing in on them.

"Look out!" someone screamed.

Tata grabbed Marcus and they dove for cover behind an enormous statue.

And then —

Kaboom!

The flaming boulder hit the street with a deafening explosion.

Small shards of rock showered over Marcus and Tata.

But the explosion had spared them.

They struggled to their feet and made their way back to the street, where a crowd had formed. He heard gasps and wails of shock.

As Tata and Marcus approached, one of Festus's guards turned around.

"The master is dead," he announced.

Marcus peered through the crowd. The boulder had left a shallow crater in the street.

And in the center, lying in a broken heap, was Festus.

Marcus looked away.

He expected to feel happy. Festus was dead!

But it turned out there was no pleasure in seeing anyone's broken body, not even the body of someone as hateful as Festus.

Marcus looked up at the roiling cloud spewing from Vesuvius.

And all he could feel was terror.

CHAPTER 14

It seemed the magistrates had listened to Festus's visitor from Rome. Within minutes, guards were rushing out of the Forum, shouting out warnings.

"Leave the city! Go directly to the gates!" they commanded.

Tata looked at Marcus with relief.

They had done their duty. And now, at last, they could leave Pompeii.

But as they soon discovered, there would be no easy escape.

Marcus and Tata joined the sea of people

streaming down the main street toward the city gates. There were rich men and slaves, parents with babies in their arms and children clutching their robes. Some dragged carts piled high with clothes and dishes and baskets. Others lugged sacks.

As they passed the gladiator barracks, Marcus glanced inside the open gates. There was a man's body lying motionless in the grass, a pillar smashed across his back. With a jolt, Marcus realized it was the lanista. Tata saw him too. But Tata quickly looked away as he tightened his grip on Marcus's hand. Cyclops must be somewhere in this crowd, Marcus realized. But Marcus was no longer afraid of him. Everyone in Pompeii was fighting the same enemy now, the most heartless killer of all: Vesuvius.

Marcus and Tata inched along with the crowd.

The sounds from the volcano were getting louder. But most frightening was the darkening sky. An enormous dark cloud had swept down from the mountain. It stretched over the city, turning the day to night. The cloud was black and boiling, and it rumbled with thunder. And then the cloud tore open.

Bits of rock fell from the sky. They were very small and light, almost like bits of ice.

Tata caught some in his hand.

"Hardened ash," Tata said.

Ping, ping, ping, they hit rooftops.

Plop, plop, plop, they splashed into fountains.

They bounced off Marcus's head and shoulders and skittered across the street.

But within minutes, the sprinkling of rocks had turned into a downpour.

The rocks pounded down, hitting the stone streets and rooftops with an earsplitting clatter.

Bam, bam, bam!

The crowd erupted in panic, pushing and elbowing, shouting. Someone shoved Marcus and he almost stumbled. An old woman fell. But the crowd stampeded over her. The rocks seemed to be getting bigger, pounding harder and harder. Dust rose up, making it hard to see.

Marcus clutched Tata's hand. He felt as though they were caught in a stampede of terrified animals.

"Hold on tight!" Tata shouted into Marcus's ear. "I want us out of this crowd!"

They pushed and squeezed their way through, dodging sharp elbows and scratching fingers. Finally, they burst their way out of the crush of screaming people. They hurried into a narrow alley.

"Too dangerous," Tata said breathlessly. "Many people are going to get trampled."

He pulled Marcus into a doorway. They pressed themselves against the wooden door, trying to escape the hail of rocks. But the downpour was even stronger now.

Tata pointed to a small temple just ahead. "We can wait there until it stops."

They pulled their tunics over their heads and waded through the river of stones.

They were just steps from the building when, *Whoosh!*

Marcus's heart stopped as he looked up.

It was a huge fireball — bigger than the one that killed Festus.

Kaboom!

The explosion knocked Marcus back. The last thing he saw before he fell was a huge chunk of rock smacking Tata in the head. Marcus hit the ground hard, but within seconds he was back on his feet. He charged over to where Tata lay crumpled on a bed of stones.

Marcus dropped to his knees, grabbing Tata's hand.

"Tata!" he cried.

But Tata just lay there, completely still.

CHAPTER 15

Tata was breathing. Marcus could see that. But then why didn't he open his eyes? Why didn't Tata answer when Marcus called his name? The rock seemed to have knocked him into a deep and terrible sleep, and Marcus could not wake him up.

The storm of rocks continued. Flaming boulders whooshed through the sky, their explosions booming all around. Somehow Marcus managed to drag Tata through the rocks. With a strength he never knew he had, he hoisted Tata up the five stairs that led through the temple's open doorway. He laid Tata on the cold stone floor and collapsed next to him.

Hours passed before Tata's eyes finally fluttered open, and even longer before the fog cleared from his eyes and he could sit up. With each passing minute, it seemed, the mountain's fury grew stronger. The booming and whooshing and thundering and pounding had melded together into a bone-rattling roar. The walls of the temple shook and groaned. They were running out of time, Marcus knew. And then suddenly Tata turned to him.

He took Marcus's hand. "My dear son, it is time for you to go," he said.

"I know," Marcus said. "As soon as you're strong enough we can —"

"No," Tata interrupted. "I'll never make it to the gates. But if you go now you'll still have a chance."

It took a moment for Marcus to understand what Tata was saying: that Marcus should escape by himself.

"No," Marcus said, locking eyes with Tata.

"Please, Marcus. I have thought about this. I have considered every idea. There is no other possibility."

Marcus knew that this was right. But it didn't matter.

"I'm sorry," Marcus said. "But I'm staying here with you."

He looked away so Tata wouldn't see his tears.

And that's when he finally took a good look at the statue that stood right in front of them.

The god with wings on his hat and on his sandals.

Marcus's whole body tingled.

The god was Mercury.

A strange but familiar voice whispered in his mind.

"When hope is lost, follow the hand of Mercury."

The words were so clear, as though the old beggar woman was still right next to him.

Marcus jumped up and went to the statue. He touched the marble, half expecting the statue to turn to flesh and blood, for Mercury to scoop him and Tata into his arms and fly them to the heavens.

"What is it?" Tata said.

He turned to Tata. "That old beggar woman, Tata," Marcus explained. "There was something else she said to me."

He spoke her words slowly to Tata.

Marcus waited for Tata to tell him it was crazy to believe in the ranting words of a stranger.

But Tata didn't shake his head. He stared at the statue intently, studying it.

And Marcus understood that at that moment it didn't matter whether the beggar woman's words were science or magic or madness. Marcus felt the truth of her words in his heart. And so, it seemed, did Tata.

Tata rose to his feet, shaking off his pain and weakness.

"Marcus," he said, his eyes wide with excitement. "Look at the statue's right hand."

Marcus saw it too. It seemed the statue was pointing to something.

But what? The floor was bare.

Unless . . .

Marcus dropped to his knees. He felt around the tile floor until he found a gap between two large tiles.

His heart pounded as he dug his fingers into the gap. There was a groove in the side of one of the tiles. He lifted it up. And he could barely believe what he saw underneath.

There was a trapdoor.

CHAPTER 16

They lifted open the door and peered into the darkness. All they could see was a rickety wooden ladder leading down into the blackness. The smell of sulfur wafted up, stinging Marcus's eyes.

"It must lead to some kind of tunnel," Tata said.

"Where does the tunnel go?" Marcus asked.

"There are tunnels under many Roman cities," Tata said. "Most lead out of the city. People used them to escape in an enemy attack."

But what if this tunnel didn't lead out of the city?

Before he could ask, Tata was climbing down the ladder. He was quickly swallowed by the pitch darkness.

Seconds later his voice echoed up from below.

"Yes, Marcus, it's a tunnel! Come quickly!"

Marcus climbed onto the ladder and fumbled his way down, down, down.

When he reached the bottom, Tata took his arm.

"This way," Tata said, turning him. "Follow closely behind me."

They moved blindly into a narrow passage, crawling on their hands and knees. It was hot as an oven and the passage was so narrow that their shoulders brushed against the rough sides. The stink of sulfur made Marcus gag. Sweat poured into his eyes. His heart hammered. The tunnel seemed endless. And the farther they went, the more terrified Marcus felt.

What if the sulfur killed them? What if the tunnel collapsed?

Marcus tried to fix his thoughts on his heroes, to gather strength from the stories that had always inspired him. He imagined he was Odysseus, braving the wild seas as he returned home from a decade of fighting. He thought of Hercules, fighting the ferocious beasts. But those stories were of no help to him now. His muscles cramped, his arms and legs shook so violently that it was hard to move. A terrifying idea took hold of him: that this tunnel would never end, that he would be forever trapped in this evil darkness. They'd never make it out.

But suddenly his mind flashed to a new story, one that was still being written.

And it was this story that gave Marcus the strength to keep moving.

It was the story of a slave boy who saved his own father by hurling a live cobra through the air, who escaped from killer clouds, leaping flames, and fiery boulders that came hurtling from the sky. He was not favored by the gods or aided by powerful kings. It was the strange words of a mysterious beggar woman that guided him. A tattered mare who carried him. And his father — so wise and good and brave — who showed him the way through the darkness.

It was this heroic boy who kept crawling through the tunnel as tears poured from his stinging eyes, who found the strength to help Tata kick open the door at the end of the tunnel. They clawed through piles of rocks to get to the surface, just outside the city gates of Pompeii. They staggered across a stone-covered field to the olive grove.

The old white mare was waiting for them.

Marcus put his face close to Peg's, looking into her gentle eye. Tata gently brushed away the rocks and ash that covered her coat.

"You waited," Marcus said.

Snort.

Of course she hadn't left them.

Marcus and Tata climbed onto Peg's back.

Without so much as a tap, the mare took off

toward Rome. She ran swiftly, her feet barely touching the ground.

They were many miles away when the cloud of ash and gas above Vesuvius collapsed down to earth. The cloud ignited, turning into a flaming whirlwind that blasted down the mountain at speeds faster than any chariot.

Within seconds, the city of Pompeii was burned and buried.

But the horror of Pompeii was now behind Marcus, and all he felt of the mountain's fury was a whisper of heat on his back.

He gripped Tata tightly, and together they looked ahead, for the bright lights of Rome.

BACK IN TIME

I'm always sad to say good-bye to my characters when I finish writing one of my I Survived books. By the time I finally polish up my last draft, my characters seem real to me — dear friends or even family. Marcus and Tata are especially close to my heart, maybe because I had to travel so far back in time to get to know them — almost two thousand years.

I kept reminding myself how very long ago it was that Pompeii was destroyed. It was before the United States was a country, before

Christopher Columbus sailed the seas, before the time of the knights and the great castles of the Middle Ages. Pompeii is in Italy. But two thousand years ago, the country of Italy didn't yet exist. Most of Europe and parts of Africa were all combined in one huge kingdom known as the Roman Empire.

In many ways, life in ancient Roman times was brutal. Slavery was common. Those horrific gladiator shows attracted thousands of delighted fans. Rome's armies were always on the march, conquering new territories and dragging home new slaves. Without medicines and vaccines, most people died young.

But in some ways, life in ancient Pompeii was surprisingly similar to our lives today. Like you and your friends, the kids of Pompeii (those who were not slaves) went to school, learned math, read stories and poems, and played sports. They loved their pet dogs. Just as you obsess over your favorite football or basketball stars, kids of Pompeii were wild about championship gladiators. There were even fast-food restaurants: Pompeii's streets were lined with little stalls that served up soup and stews and bread to people on the go.

I learned all of this during a recent visit to Pompeii. Most of the city has been uncovered and is now an enormous outdoor museum. My husband, David, and I walked through the streets, admired the fountains and statues and mosaics and the graffiti carved into the walls. I even stood in the grassy arena of Pompeii's amphitheater, where thousands of gladiators fought their brutal matches.

It was like traveling back in time, and it was on that trip that I discovered my characters. And of course I met the most frightening "character" of all: the mountain Vesuvius.

There it was, looming over Pompeii just as it did back in AD 79. Vesuvius is now silent and beautiful and green, though it is missing its top, which was blown to pieces in AD 79. But I wasn't fooled. Vesuvius remains one of the most dangerous volcanoes in the world. During my visit, I was always nervously peeking up at that big green mountain, checking for wisps of smoke.

I learned so much while I was writing this book. But as always, there is so much more I want to share with you! So I've thought about the questions that might be on your mind, and tried to come up with clear answers. I hope what you've learned in my book will inspire you to do more research, to take your own trip back in time.

I wish I could go with you.

Nunc valete! (Good-bye for now!)

QUESTIONS AND ANSWERS ABOUT POMPEII AND MOUNT VESUVIUS

How many people died in the eruption of Vesuvius?

There are no records of how many people lived in Pompeii, and how many were killed. But experts estimate that as many as twenty thousand people lived in Pompeii and in its surrounding towns. Of those, between ten thousand and sixteen thousand likely died.

Many people did escape in the first hours after the eruption. Most of those who stayed behind were likely killed by the waves of gases and fire that swept down the mountain. These *pyroclastic surges* traveled at 400 miles per hour, and instantly burned everything in their paths.

What happened to Pompeii after the eruption?

The eruption lasted for three days and buried Pompeii under thirty feet of ash and stone. Word of the disaster reached Rome, and the emperor sent a small team to investigate. But it's unlikely they — or anyone — got too close. For months afterward, the ground must have been very hot. Poisonous gases continued to seep from the earth. There were continuous earth tremors.

In the early years after the eruption, people did try to tunnel into the ruins to find their belongings — or to steal. But as the decades passed, the city was slowly forgotten.

By the year AD 500, the great Roman Empire had crumbled. Cities were invaded by "barbarians" — hordes of fighters from the north and from Asia. These invaders stole whatever they could and destroyed the rest. Most written records of history were lost. Europe was plunged into a terrible time known as the Dark Ages. There was little learning, art, or interest in science and history. People struggled to simply survive during a time of fear and superstition.

How was Pompeii rediscovered?

Many, many centuries passed. The mountain "healed" from the eruption. Grass and trees grew back. People slowly returned to the areas around the mountain. Farmers once again planted olive groves and farms on the slopes. The Dark Ages ended.

By the 1600s, new cities had been born all around Europe and a few bold settlers had headed across the Atlantic Ocean to a strange land called America. People in Europe were interested in learning and discovery again. Many became fascinated by the ancient Roman civilization that had vanished. Around Vesuvius, there were rumors of a beautiful city that once stretched out below the mountain. Every so often a well digger or farmer would discover an intriguing artifact — the arm of a statue, a chunk of a mosaic.

But it wasn't until the year 1764 — nearly 1,700 years after the eruption — when one of the greatest Pompeii discoveries was made: the ruins of a beautiful temple. More dazzling artifacts were soon found.

The early diggers were more interested in snatching whatever treasure they could dig up. But by the 1800s, people realized that Pompeii's artifacts must be preserved and studied. Today, most of Pompeii's treasures are in museums. Excavations of the city have continued steadily ever since, though today at least one quarter of the city is still buried.

Why is Pompeii so important?

There are other places where you can see ruins of buildings from ancient Roman times. The city of Rome is filled with them. But there is no place in the world like Pompeii, which was buried in AD 79 and sealed for centuries, like a time capsule.

The ash and stone preserved more than just the buildings. Archeologists have unearthed thousands of artifacts — skeletons, petrified loaves of bread, statues, toys, furniture, chariots, gladiator helmets, silverware, cooking pots, shoes, earrings, and much, much more.

Most of what we know about life in ancient Rome comes from the discoveries made in Pompeii and a neighboring town called Herculaneum, which was also buried by Vesuvius in AD 79.

Will Vesuvius erupt again?

Yes.

Vesuvius is one of the world's most dangerous volcanoes — and also one of the most closely monitored. It has erupted many times over the past few centuries. None of those eruptions were nearly as powerful as the one that buried Pompeii. But experts have no doubt that another enormous eruption could happen soon.

And this disaster could be devastating. Today, an estimated two million people live in the dangerous "red zone" around Vesuvius. Just fifteen miles north is the crowded city of Naples, where nearly one million people live.

Hopefully, the mountain would give plenty of warning before a major eruption, and people would have time to evacuate. But today, nearly two thousand years after Pompeii was destroyed, we remain powerless against the destructive fury of a major volcanic eruption. Much of this beautiful region of Italy would likely be buried again.

And about the date, AD 79 . . . ?

You might wonder what those letters "AD" stand for.

Today, most of the world uses a calendar that

divides history into two big time periods — the time before Jesus Christ was born and the time after. The time before "year zero" is known as BC, which stands for "before Christ." The time after is known as AD. Many people believe that stands for "after death" — because that would make sense. But AD is actually an abbreviation for the Latin words *Anno Domini*, which mean "in the year of our Lord," indicating the time after Jesus was born. These terms came into use as Christianity spread across many parts of the world. Nowadays, you might see the terms BCE and CE used instead, which mean "Before the Common (or Current) Era" and "in the Common Era."

FOR FURTHER READING
AND LEARNING

My bookshelf is now groaning under the weight of dozens of amazing books about ancient Rome, Pompeii, gladiators, and volcanoes. Here are some of the books I discovered for readers your age.

Ashen Sky: The Letters of Pliny the Younger on the Eruption of Vesuvius, by Pliny, illustrated by Barry Moser
Pliny the Younger was a seventeen-year-old boy when he witnessed the eruption of Mount Vesuvius in AD 79. Years later, he described what he saw in two letters, which are the only eyewitness accounts we have of that eruption.

Bodies in the Ash: Life and Death in Ancient Pompeii, by James M. Deem
Lots of great info about the disaster and the rediscovery of Pompeii.

Eruption! Volcanoes and the Science of Saving Lives, by Elizabeth Rusch, photographs by Tom Uhlman

A thrilling look at some of today's most dangerous volcanoes, and the men and women who study them.

The Buried City of Pompeii, by Shelley Tanaka

An amazing book about Pompeii and the AD 79 eruption, with beautiful illustrations and photographs, and a glimpse into the lives of people who might have lived in the city.

The Secrets of Vesuvius, by Sara C. Bisel

An archeologist shares her experience studying skeletons found in Herculaneum, the town also buried by Vesuvius.

THE *NEW YORK TIMES* BESTSELLING SERIES

I SURVIVED

THE JAPANESE TSUNAMI, 2011

by Lauren Tarshis

SCHOLASTIC

I SURVIVED

THE JAPANESE TSUNAMI, 2011

by Lauren Tarshis

illustrated by Scott Dawson

Scholastic Inc.

CHAPTER 1

MARCH 11, 2011

2:46 P.M.

SHOGAHAMA, JAPAN

At first, the wave was tiny.

It was just a ripple in the huge Pacific Ocean.

But it moved quickly, faster than a jet.

And as it got closer to Japan's coast, it got bigger. It grew and grew, until it was a monstrous wall of water, dozens of feet high, hundreds of miles long. It destroyed everything in its path.

The wave smashed into crowded cities, knocking down buildings, swallowing factories, chewing up highways and bridges. It washed away beautiful villages, flattening pine forests and turning rice fields into seas of mud and garbage. In quiet fishing towns, boats tumbled like dice into the streets, smashing into shops and homes.

Eleven-year-old Ben Kudo saw the wave coming as he stood on a street in the tiny village of Shogahama. At first, it looked to him as if a cloud of smoke was rising up over the ocean.

Was it a ship on fire?

But then a siren blared.

Terrified voices shouted out.

Ben didn't speak Japanese. But he understood one word.

Tsunami!

Seconds later, the huge, foaming black wave crashed into the shore.

Ben and his family thought they could race away from the wave in a car. But the water caught them. And suddenly, Ben was all by himself. The wave grabbed Ben and sucked him under. The churning water twisted him, tore at him, spun him around like a bird caught in a tornado.

Terror screamed through his body.

He was drowning!

He fought with all his might, but the water wouldn't let him go. It was as though he was in the jaws of a ferocious monster.

And there was no escape.

CHAPTER 2

The score was tied with ten seconds to go. Ben grabbed the ball and dribbled down the court. He zigzagged around guys who seemed ten feet tall. The crowd cheered. As usual, Dad's voice rose up above the rest.

"You can do it, Ben!"

The clock was counting down —

4, 3, 2 . . .

Ben shot the ball.

It sailed for the basket and hung in the air. . . .

Ben's eyes flew open.

He sat straight up in bed, drenched with sweat, breathing hard. It took him a few seconds to remember that he wasn't at home in California. He was at his uncle's house, in the tiny village of Shogahama, Japan.

His five-year-old brother, Harry, had been asleep next to Ben. Now Harry was up, too.

"Scary dream?" Harry asked, putting a little hand on Ben's clammy back.

Ben shrugged off Harry's hand.

"Not too bad," Ben said, careful to keep his voice from shaking.

He never wanted Harry to know that he felt sad or scared.

And besides, a dream about Dad was never a bad dream.

It was waking up that was torture — remembering all over again that Dad was gone. He had died four months ago, in a car accident near the California air force base where they lived. Dad had been an F-16 pilot for the U.S. Air Force. He'd flown dangerous missions all over the world. And he'd died on a California highway, on his way home from picking up a box of doughnuts for Ben and Harry.

A few months before the accident, Dad had announced a big surprise: a family trip to Shogahama, the fishing village in Japan where Dad had lived until he was ten. They would go in March, during Ben's school vacation. They would stay with Dad's Uncle Tomeo; they all called him *Ojisan*, the Japanese word for uncle.

Ben had always dreamed of visiting Shogahama. Ojisan was more like a grandfather to him than a far-away uncle. He'd come to visit them in California several times over the years. Ben had heard so many stories about Dad's life growing up in the village. He couldn't wait to see it for himself.

But not without Dad.

Ben couldn't believe it when his mom announced they were still taking the trip. He'd begged her to cancel, but Mom never changed her mind. "Don't be tricked by that sweet smile," Dad used to say. Mom had been in the air force, too, before she had Ben.

"She's tougher than all of us," Dad always said with a proud smile.

Mom wanted to go to Shogahama. And so here they were.

Harry got out of bed, his Darth Vader pajamas drooping on his bony shoulders. Ojisan's cat, Nya, was asleep at the foot of the mattress. Harry scooped her up. The cat had to be a hundred years old, her black fur rubbed away in places.

She was small and scrawny with a crooked tail that looked like the letter *z*. Instead of saying, "meow," she had a shriek that hurt Ben's ears.

"Eee! Eee!"

Ben wished Harry would ignore the cat so she would leave them alone. But Harry had decided that Nya was a Jedi cat, Darth Vader's special assistant. And somehow the old cat didn't mind being dragged around the house as Harry played his Star Wars games, chasing invisible enemies with his lightsaber.

Now Harry rubbed his cheek against Nya's head and looked at Ben with his bright eyes.

"Will you help me climb the tree after breakfast?" he asked. "I need to make my wish."

Not that again.

One of the stories Dad told about Shogahama was that the cherry trees were magic. If you climbed to the top of a tree, Dad said, you could make a wish.

Ben knew Dad was just telling fairy tales. But Harry believed in everything. For the whole week, Harry had been eyeing the cherry tree in Ojisan's small front yard, waiting for the rain to stop so he could climb to the top. Now the sky was bright blue, and Harry was ready.

"You know what I'm going to wish for?" Harry said, leaning in close. His coppery eyes sparkled. "I'm going to wish for Daddy to come back to us."

The words hit Ben right in the throat.

"Harry," he said sharply. "You know Dad is gone, and you can't bring him back."

Tears sprang into Harry's eyes.

"You'll see!" he cried, turning and running out of the room with Nya tight in his arms.

Suddenly Ben was crying, too.

He stood up quickly, angrily wiping away his tears as he pulled himself together.

Ben had to be tough, like Dad.

During Dad's last tour in Afghanistan, when

Ben was a baby, the engine of Dad's F-16 exploded. He had to eject from the plane over enemy territory. He broke his ankle when he parachuted down. But he still managed to escape into the mountains before enemy fighters found him. For six days, he'd hidden in a cave, until he was finally rescued by a helicopter filled with U.S. Marines.

Ben could picture Dad, standing in the darkness with steely eyes, never once stopping to moan or cry.

And that's how Ben was determined to be.

He went to find Harry. He guessed there was no harm in helping him climb a tree.

But Ben was too late.

He was walking toward the kitchen door when he heard Harry scream.

He ran outside, and there was his little brother, lying in a heap under the cherry tree.

He was covered in blood.

CHAPTER 3

Ben stood between Mom and Ojisan as the doctor looked Harry over. Ben's stomach was still twisted in knots from the sight of Harry lying on the ground. The little guy looked terrible — a blood-crusted nose and a big gash on his arm.

But as battered as he looked, he wasn't so badly hurt. It seemed that the branches of the tree had slowed Harry's fall before he hit the dirt, and that the ground was soft from all the rain. The doctor — his name was Dr. Sato — checked Harry over very carefully. When he was finished, he put his hand on Harry's head.

"You must be made of rubber, Harry," he said in perfect English. "Did you bounce when you hit the ground?"

"I think so!" Harry exclaimed.

This made them all laugh, even Ben. The sound that came out of his mouth surprised him, it had been so long since he'd heard it.

"I just need to fix up that little cut on your arm," Dr. Sato said. "It will just take a few stitches."

Uh-oh.

"Nooooo!" screamed Harry.

Show Harry a cobra and he'd smile and reach out to pet it. But the tiniest needle sent him into fits of total panic.

Dr. Sato wasn't going to get anywhere near Harry, Ben was sure.

Except it turned out Dr. Sato was a genius.

"Mrs. Kudo," Dr. Sato said to Mom, raising his voice above Harry's screams. "Is it true that Darth Vader has a scar on his arm?"

Harry stopped crying.

"Yes," Mom said, putting on a serious face. "Isn't that right, Ben?"

"Totally," Ben answered, trying not to smile. "He got it in a lightsaber fight."

They all looked at Harry, who finally took a deep, hiccupping breath.

"Can I get a scar?" he asked softly.

"If you sit perfectly still while I do the stitches," Dr. Sato said.

Harry held out his arm to the doctor.

"Go ahead." He sniffed bravely.

Forty-five minutes later, Harry admired his sewn-up cut as if it was the best birthday present ever. They all said good-bye to Dr. Sato.

They piled into Ojisan's little car and headed back to Shogahama. The road was narrow, and curved around high rocky cliffs. Out one window, Pacific waves crashed against a wall of craggy rocks. On the other side, the view stretched across rice fields to the mountains, which towered up to the clear blue sky.

"Daddy was right," Mom said. "I think this is the most beautiful place on Earth."

"You should stay longer," Ojisan said.

"I want to!" Harry shouted.

Not Ben. He was glad they were leaving in two days.

He'd miss Ojisan. But being here had turned Ben all soft. He'd been dreaming about Dad every night, thinking about him all the time.

Back home, Ben managed to keep his mind clear.

It wasn't easy. He'd given up basketball, even quitting the travel team he'd worked so hard to make. Hoops had been *their* game — Ben and Dad's. After the accident, just the sound of a bouncing ball would hit Ben in the chest like a bullet.

He'd cleaned out his room so there were no more pictures of Dad. He'd ripped down the F-16 poster that had hung over his bed. When Mom knocked on his locked door, Ben said he was doing homework. When Harry wanted to play, Ben told him to go away.

Sometimes it seemed that Ben had turned his room into a cave, a dark space like where Dad hid after he was shot down in Afghanistan. Yeah, it was lonely in there sometimes.

But at least in his cave, Ben felt safe.

CHAPTER 4

2:40 P.M.

Harry was exhausted from the trip to the hospital. Mom helped him change out of his blood-spattered pajamas and tucked him into bed. A minute later he was asleep, with Nya curled up on his stomach.

Ben was in the kitchen pouring some juice when Ojisan came in.

"How about a walk?" he said quietly.

"No thanks, Ojisan," Ben said with a tinge of guilt. "I'm kind of tired, too."

Every day they'd been here, Ojisan had invited Ben to go exploring. And every day, Ben had thought of an excuse. Ben didn't want to see the pine forest where Dad used to play hide-and-seek, or the marina where Dad learned to fish. He didn't want to hear any of Ojisan's stories about Dad.

Ben slinked out of the kitchen, avoiding Ojisan's eyes.

He'd just stepped into the bedroom when Harry suddenly sat up.

Harry had a dreamy look on his face. Ben wondered if he was fully awake.

"You know," he said softly, "I made it to the tippy top."

"Top of what?" Ben asked, sitting down next to Harry.

"The cherry tree," Harry answered. "Before I fell down, I made the wish, Ben. I made the wish!"

His eyes were glowing.

Before Ben could say anything, Nya suddenly jumped up and yowled. She stood there with her fur standing straight up, then started pushing against Harry's arm with her nose. It looked as if she wanted to roll Harry off the bed.

Was the old cat going totally bonkers?

And then there was a strange sound, a very deep rumbling.

The glass of water on the dresser jiggled.

At first, Ben thought it was fighter jets passing overhead, like at home when a squadron returned to the base.

But the rumbling got louder and louder, and the bed began to shake.

"Ben!" Harry cried. "What is it?"

Dread rose up in Ben.

Ojisan shouted from somewhere across the house.

"Ben! Harry! *Dishin! Dishin!*"

Ben didn't need to understand Japanese to know what Ojisan was saying.

Earthquake!

The shaking got stronger and stronger until Ben and Harry were bouncing up and down on the bed.

Ben gripped Harry as hard as he could so they wouldn't fall off.

It was as though they were rafting on a wild river.

Thud!

The dresser tipped over.

Smash!

The lamp hit the floor, its lightbulb exploding with a shattering *pop*.

"EEEEE!" screeched Nya.

But above all the other sounds was a thundering roar, like the earth itself was screaming with fury. The sound hammered into Ben's ears and pounded his brain.

"Make it stop!" screamed Harry.

But there was no stopping it. Ben didn't know that earthquakes could last so long. The ground in California shook all the time. But never for more than a few seconds. And never like this! Ben suddenly remembered that more earthquakes happen in Japan than practically anywhere else on Earth, even California. In Science, they learned about the earthquake that destroyed Tokyo in the 1920s, and another one in the city of Kobe, in the 1990s.

How could he have forgotten all that?

They'd also learned how skyscrapers in Japan were built to survive strong earthquakes. The tall buildings here were made to sway, like blades of grass on a windy day.

But the buildings around here looked old. Ojisan's house was made of wood and plaster. Like all the houses here, the roof was covered with red clay tiles.

Could Ojisan's house survive an earthquake like this?

The answer came with a *BOOM* that rose up above the other noises.

"Ben, look!" Harry cried, pointing up.

A huge crack had appeared in the ceiling. It got bigger and bigger.

Any second, the ceiling would collapse.

They had to get out of here!

CHAPTER 5

Ben grabbed Harry. He crawled across the floor toward the door, dragging Harry along with him. He pushed against the door. But it was stuck. It was wedged against the cracked, broken floor.

Now what? They were trapped!

Panic churned Ben's insides. They couldn't stay here! But where could they go? His body was frozen. His heart pounded. His mind swirled so that it was impossible to think.

Was this how Dad had felt, when he knew his F-16 was going to crash?

Dad had only recently told Ben the story of the crash. They'd been at the basketball court across from their house. Normally, Dad didn't tell stories about being at war. But something about the *thump, thump, thump* of the basketball had loosened Dad up, got him talking.

He'd described what had happened when the engine exploded, when the lights on the cockpit console had flashed like a video game gone haywire. He was twenty-five thousand feet in the air, rocketing through the sky at five hundred miles per hour. Any minute, the entire plane could burst into flames. His only chance was to eject, to pull the big yellow lever that would explode him out of the plane and send him shooting through the endless sky.

The roof of the cockpit — the canopy — was made of clear plastic, and was designed to pop

247

off when the eject lever was pulled. A small explosive under Dad's seat would blast the entire seat into the air. Two parachutes would open — the first to yank Dad upright, the second to float him down to Earth.

But what if the canopy didn't open and Dad crushed his head? What if the parachutes failed and he fell like a rock straight into the ground? Dad had heard stories about ejections that went horribly wrong. Plenty of pilots had died, or were so badly hurt that they never walked again.

These were terrifying thoughts. But Dad had been trained for these life-and-death moments — to fly through enemy fire, to land on an aircraft carrier in a thunderstorm, to avoid a missile aimed straight for the belly of his jet.

"The fear is always there," Dad had told Ben, bouncing the ball and lining up at the free-throw line. "But you can't let it take over."

He'd eyed the basket and taken a shot.

"You have to choose: live or die. If you let yourself panic, you're finished."

Swish.

Now Ben remembered what Dad had said to him next.

"What you learn in training is to close your eyes," Dad had said. "You breathe deep. You breathe, and breathe, and breathe. And somehow your mind clears so you can do what you need to do."

Ben closed his eyes now. It was hard to fill his lungs — his chest felt as if it was wrapped tight in rubber bands. But he kept thinking of Dad's words:

Breathe.

Breathe.

Breathe.

And somehow his mind stopped swirling. His body relaxed.

And then, almost without thinking, Ben grabbed Harry.

He dragged him back toward the bed, which had strong metal legs.

Ben pushed Harry underneath, and then scrambled in after him.

"Wait!" Harry screamed. "Nya!"

The cat was in the middle of the room, frozen in shock.

Harry tried to crawl out, but Ben gripped on to his ankle, pulling Harry back in.

"Get her!" Harry screamed at Ben.

Ben slid out from under the bed and crawled on his elbows after Nya. He caught her by the tail. She howled and scratched at him, but he managed to pull her back so that Harry could grab her.

Ben had barely made it under the bed when the room seemed to explode.

And the ceiling came crashing down.

CHAPTER 6

Finally the shaking stopped.

It was pitch-dark. Except for Harry's soft cries, everything was completely silent.

"Ben?" Harry said, his voice barely a whimper.

"We're okay," Ben said.

And somehow they were. As the dust settled, Ben could see wreckage all over the floor — broken roof tiles, huge chunks of wood and plaster. The bed had protected them.

The panic started to creep back, cold hands climbing up Ben's spine. His mind began to swirl with questions.

Where were Mom and Ojisan?

What had happened to the rest of the house?

He and Harry had managed to survive the shaking. But what if Mom and Ojisan hadn't found a safe place? What if the earthquake started again? What if . . .

He closed his eyes again and took a deep breath, than another. His thoughts slowed down enough for Ben to remember that Mom had been trained by the air force, just like Dad. She knew how to take care of herself. And Ojisan had built this house himself. He'd know where they would be safe.

Harry huddled close to Ben, crying hard.

"I'm scared," he sobbed. Ben patted his back and tried to comfort him. But Harry was screaming now, worse than when Dr. Sato told him he'd need stitches. Patting him on the back wasn't working.

"Jedi knights have to be strong," Ben said. "Now that you have a scar, you have to be brave."

That seemed to work.

Harry gave a big sniff.

He wiped his nose on his sleeve.

He snuggled Nya close. "We have to be brave, Nya," he whispered.

A moment later, there were footsteps.

"Ben! Harry!"

"Mom!" Harry shrieked.

"Boys, are you hurt?" she called, her voice ringing clear and strong through the dust.

"We're okay!" Ben shouted, trying to sound braver than he felt. "We're under the bed!"

"Stay where you are!" Ojisan called. Their uncle was there, too!

———

It seemed like forever before Mom and Ojisan
were able to clear a path through the wreckage.
But soon they were in the bedroom. And there
was Mom, on her knees, peering under the bed
at Ben and Harry. Her face was streaked with
dirt and sweat, but her eyes were filled with relief.

"You can come out now," she told them.

Ben pushed Harry into Mom's arms, and Ben
climbed out after him.

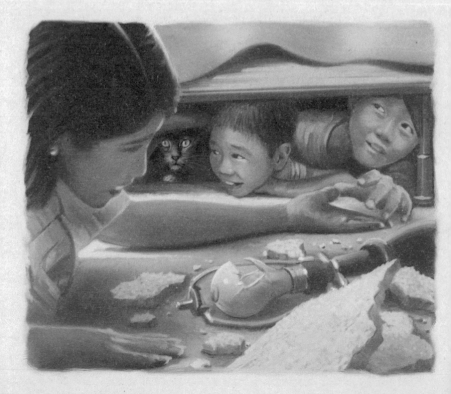

Mom wrapped her arms around both of them. Lately, Ben had pulled away from Mom's hugs. Not now. He could hear Mom's heart pounding through her thick sweater. Nya crawled out and buried her head in Harry's leg.

"That was very smart, to hide under the bed," Mom said, letting the boys go so she could look at them.

"Ben took us there," Harry said, picking up Nya again.

Mom looked at Ben. She reached out and touched his cheek, and he felt a flush of unexpected pride.

But there was no time to talk. Mom found Harry's shoes and helped him put them on.

"Come," Ojisan said, plucking Nya from the floor and handing her to Harry. "We need to get outside. That was a very strong earthquake. It is the strongest I have ever felt. There will be more shaking. It is not safe in the house."

As if the earth itself had heard Ojisan, there was a sharp rumble that brought another piece of ceiling crashing to the floor.

They hurried through the house, stepping over fallen furniture, piles of books, and broken glass. The rest of the house was still standing, but it looked as if it could come down any second. Ben was relieved to get outside. They made their way across the yard and into the street. Some big trees had fallen, but Ojisan's cherry tree was still standing.

"Wait here," Ojisan said. He hurried to the middle of the street, where a group of his neighbors was gathered. Three of the houses on the road were completely wrecked. But it seemed as though everyone was safe.

Mom, Ben, and Harry huddled together in the cold. Harry held Nya tight.

"The worst is over," Mom said.

Yes, Ben told himself. Nothing could be as bad as that earthquake.

But then Ben noticed that Ojisan had drifted to the edge of the street. He was standing with two other men. They were all looking intently at the ocean in the distance.

Ben followed the path of their gaze until he figured out what they were looking at: a strange gray cloud hovering over the ocean.

It looked almost like smoke.

Was a big ship on fire?

No, that didn't make sense. No ship was that big.

A siren blared.

And with a sudden jolt, Ben understood that it wasn't a cloud.

It wasn't a fire.

It was a wave.

A gigantic wave, taller than a building, and so wide he couldn't see where it started or ended. It seemed to stretch endlessly across the ocean.

Ojisan shouted.

"Tsunami!"

CHAPTER 7

There was no time to think.

"Get to the car!" Ojisan shouted.

Mom picked up Harry and they all sprinted to the car and jumped in. Mom pulled Harry onto her lap in the front; Ben threw himself into the back.

Ojisan had the engine running even before Ben had closed his door. The car screeched out of the driveway.

Why was Ojisan panicking? Why was everyone running? They weren't very close to the ocean — it was at least a five-minute walk. Ben had never heard of a wave traveling so far inland.

Probably Ojisan just didn't want to take any chances.

The road had been split apart by the earthquake. Ojisan had to swerve around the cracks. Ben flew from side to side in the backseat until he managed to put on his seat belt.

"What's happening?" Harry cried, hugging Nya so tight Ben worried the cat's head would pop off.

"We're just moving away from the ocean," Mom said in her usual calm voice.

There was a strange noise. It rose up suddenly, a roar louder even than the earthquake. This time it seemed as if jets were landing right behind them.

Ben turned, and what he saw almost stopped his heart:

A frothing wall of water, rushing up the street.

And it wasn't just water. The wave carried parts of houses, a smashed car, an entire pine tree, slabs of wood and metal. It was devouring everything in its path. Two men were running on the sidewalk. Ben gasped as the wave swallowed them whole.

And now the wave was coming for them.

Ojisan stomped on the gas pedal. The engine whined, and the car zoomed forward.

Mom reached back and grabbed Ben's hand, squeezing it tight. Their eyes locked. At first Ben couldn't read the expression on Mom's face, because he'd never seen it before, not even in the days after Dad's accident.

Mom was scared.

And suddenly there was water all around them, foaming black water, rising up in angry waves.

The car spun wildly as the waves rushed up around the tires.

Time seemed to stop.

The car tipped sharply in the rising water. Ben was held tight by his seat belt. Mom and Harry toppled onto Ojisan, and they all crashed together into his door.

The door popped open. Ojisan fell out of the car.

"Ojisan!" Ben screamed.

And now Mom and Harry were about to fall out, too! The car door was swung wide open, and Mom and Harry teetered in the doorway. Mom clung to the steering wheel with one hand, and kept her other arm around Harry, who gripped Nya.

Ben jumped forward to grab Mom, but his seat belt choked him back.

"Mom!" Ben shouted. "Hold on!"

"I'm trying!" Mom said.

Ben struggled with his seat belt, and finally got it open. But before he could grab hold of

Mom, the car tipped all the way to the side, almost all the way over. Mom, Harry, and Nya tumbled out.

Ben watched in horror as the water swept them away.

Ben tried to climb over the seats, to dive out after them.

But the water was higher now, thrashing the car back and forth. The door slammed shut. Waves crashed over the roof of the car. Freezing water gushed in, surrounding Ben. In seconds, it was up to his chest. Ben tried to open the door, but it wouldn't budge.

The water was at his chin now.

And there was no way out.

CHAPTER 8

The car spun and flipped as it sank deeper and deeper. It became pitch-dark, and Ben got so dizzy he couldn't tell which way was up and which was down.

It was like being in a locked box filled with water or . . . a plane.

A fighter jet that had crashed into the ocean.

Ben remembered the stories Dad had told him about pilot training. It took years to learn to be an F-16 pilot. And the training never ended. There were always new formations to learn, different drills to practice. The worst, Dad said, were the water survival drills.

Every military pilot is trained so they can survive in a water crash. A plane sinks quickly, and fills with water in seconds. Even the best pilot will get completely confused under the water, just like Ben felt now.

And so the air force puts its pilots through practice drills. Twice a year, Dad went to a special training center where he was blindfolded, strapped into a fake cockpit, flipped over, and dunked into a freezing-cold pool. He had to unstrap, find an exit, and swim to the surface — all while holding his breath. In his early years, Dad sometimes failed the test. A rescue diver had to fish him out and drag him to the surface.

But there was no rescue diver waiting for Ben now.

He would escape, or he would drown.

Ben closed his eyes and remembered what Dad had said about escaping from a sunken plane: how pilots turned their hands into eyes, how they would feel their way through the plane until they found a way out. Doors don't work in a sinking plane; the pressure of the water seals them shut. Pilots need to find a hole, or break a window.

The water was past Ben's mouth now, brushing against his nose. He lifted his chin and took a deep breath, knowing it would be his last until he got to the surface. His hands fumbled blindly along the surfaces of the car. He tried to picture what he was feeling — the seat, the roof, the window. He found the window button, but nothing happened when he pushed it. The car's electricity must have stopped working in the water.

Now he had just a few seconds left. His lungs felt as if they were going to explode. He was losing strength. He groped until he found the steering wheel. There wasn't much room in Ojisan's tiny car, but he managed to pull his knees to his chest, and swing his body around. With all his might, he kicked at the window of the passenger door.

Boom.

The window didn't budge.

He kicked again, and again.

Boom.

Boom.

Boom.

CRACK!

Ben gave one last kick, and the glass popped out of the frame.

He turned and squirmed through the opening, fighting the force of the water gushing into the car. He pushed against the car with both feet, and rocketed up to the surface.

But he had barely taken one breath when he was sucked under again.

The water seemed to be alive, with powerful arms that thrashed Ben, tore at him. Each time he fought his way to the surface to take a breath, the water grabbed him and pulled him down again.

He couldn't keep this up, he knew. The water was winning.

And then he caught a glimpse of something big bobbing in the water, just a few feet away. He had no idea what it was. For a second, he imagined it was a whale. Ben threw his body forward, kicking with every ounce of energy he had left.

It was a couch!

Ben managed to pull himself up.

He gulped in the air, filling his aching lungs again and again.

His mouth and nose were filled with the disgusting water. He spit and coughed and blew out his nose, trying to get rid of the bitter chemical taste. He blinked his eyes, which felt as though they had been burned.

Slowly, Ben caught his breath. His vision cleared.

He looked around him, unable to believe that what he was seeing was real.

For as far as he could see, there was water — a churning black soup choked with shredded wood, slabs of glass and metal, and other wreckage.

Ben tipped his head back and screamed.

"Mom!" he shouted. "Ojisan! Harry!"

His voice echoed out, and nobody called back.

There was not another person anywhere to be seen.

The wave had swept them all away.

CHAPTER 9

Minutes passed, and Ben floated on the couch, his face buried in his arms. The blue sky of the morning had turned a dark, bruised gray. The water had calmed, the churning had stopped. Now Ben just drifted along, like a castaway in the middle of the sea. He had never felt so cold in his life.

Or so alone. Ben hadn't even felt this alone in those first weeks after Dad's accident, when he had locked himself away in his room. He had refused to see or talk to anyone, even Ojisan, who had stayed for weeks after Dad's funeral. But in that lonely darkness, Ben had known that Mom was never far from him. There was always Harry knocking on his door, his coach and his friends ringing the doorbell. Ben had sent them all away. But now he understood how important it had been, knowing that all those people were there for him.

Waiting.

Now there was nobody.

A bitter wind blew. Ben shivered. His teeth chattered so loudly that at first he didn't hear the high-pitched sound drifting from somewhere nearby.

Eee, eee.

Ben looked up, sure he was hearing things.

But there it was again.

Eee, eee.

He searched the water. Objects floated by: a lamp, newspapers, a huge stuffed teddy bear, bottles, papers, a soccer ball.

And about ten feet away, something tiny moved slowly on the water, floating on top of a mattress. At first Ben thought he was looking at a ragged stuffed animal.

But then he noticed the z-shaped tail.

And he heard the noise again.

"Eee, eee!"

Nya!

Before he could stop himself, Ben leaped into the water.

He swam as quickly as he could, blazing a trail through the wreckage.

He reached the mattress and grabbed hold.

"Nya! It's me, Ben!"

The cat stood there, shivering, staring at him with cloudy blue eyes.

"Don't you recognize me?"

He'd gone crazy now, Ben realized, if he was talking to a cat.

A cat that probably had no idea who he was.

But then he saw a kind of flash in Nya's eyes. She limped to the edge of the mattress, and put her nose right up to his face. And she started to purr.

Tears sprang into Ben's eyes as Nya nuzzled him. He felt such a rush of relief, as though this scrawny old cat was a helicopter filled with marines coming to his rescue.

He hoisted himself up onto the mattress, and sat with his legs crossed. He lifted Nya and held her against his chest, the way Harry always held her.

It was the first second of calm he'd felt since the earthquake.

But it didn't last.

Because suddenly the water was moving again. The mattress was being carried through the water, fast. Only this time the water was flowing in the opposite direction — toward the sea.

What was happening?

Ben thought about a trip to the coast the family had taken last summer, one of the best weekends they'd ever had. Mom and Harry had built a gigantic sand castle on the beach. Dad and Ben had bodysurfed for hours, riding giant waves to shore. When the waves lost power, the water would get sucked back out to sea. The current was so powerful that Dad had to hold Ben so he didn't get swept away.

That's what was happening now.

The giant wave had lost power. It was being sucked back into the ocean.

And it was taking Ben and Nya with it.

The mattress plowed through the water, pushing through piles of wreckage.

Think! Ben told himself.

Soon they would be out to sea!

Just ahead, he saw something — a tall, skinny tree poking up through the water. It was his only chance. He'd have a split second to jump off the mattress and grab the tree.

Ben lifted Nya, and put her around the back of his neck, like a scarf.

"Hold on to me," he told her.

He rose up, crouching low on the mattress. Nya dug her claws into his shoulders. But Ben didn't flinch. He kept his eye on the tree, knowing that the timing had to be perfect.

He counted down in his mind, like the numbers on a basketball shot clock:

5, 4, 3, 2, 1 . . .

He jumped off the mattress. Nya sprang off of his back and latched onto the tree. Ben reached out and tried to grab hold. But he couldn't get a good grip. His frozen hands slid across the slippery bark.

And the water took hold of him and started pulling him away.

CHAPTER 10

And then something stabbed him in the back.

He thought he'd been hit by a piece of glass.

But it was Nya. She had her front paws on Ben, and her back claws still anchored to the tree. Nya was trying to hold him in place!

It felt as if ten curved nails were hooked into his skin. But Ben gritted his teeth, and forced his icy fingers to cling to the tree. He swung his legs, wrapping them tightly around the trunk. Bit by bit, he shimmied up, so his body was out of the water.

He'd made it.

Nya unhooked from him, and climbed up the tree so that she was resting on Ben's shoulder.

"Thank you, Nya," he gasped.

Crazy kid, talking to a cat again.

Ben clung to the tree as the water rushed back to the ocean.

It was shocking how quickly the water went away, as if it was draining from a gigantic bathtub. It had to be more than twenty feet deep in places. But within minutes, it was all gone.

In its place was a sea of mud — knee-deep, black, and oily. There was a terrible smell — a rotten, poisonous stench — that burned Ben's nose.

Ben and Nya climbed down from the tree. Ben stared at the heaps of wreckage piled everywhere. There was so much wood and metal, crushed roof tiles, and bits of houses and buildings that had been chewed up by the wave. And there were things, clothes and books and magazines, an armless doll and a crushed baseball cap, a smashed laptop computer.

What about the people who had bought these things, who had worn the clothes and turned those pages, who had played with the doll and looked up basketball scores on that computer?

Where were those people?

Was Ben the only person left?

A dark feeling came over him, blacker than the wave.

Ben had never felt more tired, or more cold. His muddy clothes were frozen to his body. His bones had turned to icicles. His body was raked with gashes and cuts.

His strength was gone. He was out of ideas. He wanted to curl up in the mud. Yes, that's what he needed to do. Close his eyes. Forget all this.

But suddenly Dad flashed into his mind.

He remembered what Dad had told him about his last night in the cave in Afghanistan.

"I was in bad shape," Dad had said.

He was freezing cold, starving, and exhausted. His ankle throbbed, and was swollen to the size of a melon. The cave was crawling with rats, and Dad had hardly slept. He'd eaten some leaves that made his lips swell and his throat burn. He had no water. His radio was out of battery power. He'd been trying to send a signal all week, and had heard some crackling voices on the other end. But he had no idea who those voices belonged to, whether help was on the way or not.

"Things did not look good," Dad had said. "They did not look good at all. But here's one thing they don't teach you in training, that you just have to know in your heart. You have to know that no matter how scared you are, no matter how hopeless things seem, you simply cannot give up hope."

And Dad didn't.

He killed a rat and cooked it for dinner. He kept his mind clear by thinking of Mom and Ben, and the happy times ahead of them. He swung his arms in circles to keep blood flowing through his fingers.

On the morning of the seventh day, Dad woke up to the sound of a helicopter thundering overhead. He was too weak to walk. So he crawled out of the cave.

He made it out just in time to see the helicopter overhead, just in time to fire his signal gun.

Just in time to be saved.

Ben closed his eyes and took deep breaths until his mind felt calmer. He scanned the wreckage for something — anything — that would be useful. He finally glimpsed a can of some kind. It was fruit juice. He cleaned off the top and guzzled down half of it. He poured the rest into one of his dirty hands so Nya could lap it up.

He was still thirsty, but the juice gave him a flicker of strength.

Ben lifted Nya. He held her up so he could look into her cloudy blue eyes.

For the first time he wondered how she had survived the wave, how she'd gotten herself onto that mattress, how she'd made sure someone found her.

Harry had been right about Nya. She was as tough as a Jedi warrior.

"We're going to find them, right?" he said to her, not caring anymore that it was crazy to talk to a cat.

"Eee, eee," Nya said.

Ben decided that meant yes.

Ben carefully draped Nya around his neck.

He turned away from the ocean, and pointed himself toward the mountains.

And he walked.

CHAPTER 11

EARLY THE NEXT MORNING
SHOGAHAMA ELEMENTARY SCHOOL

Ben lay wrapped in blankets on the floor of a school gym. Nya slept on his stomach. They both shivered. There was no power at the school, and it was dark except for the glow of a few flashlights. Ben made out the shapes of people around him: at least fifty of them, laid out on straw mats or blankets. There were very old people, older than Ojisan, and young people, mothers with babies, men by themselves. People spoke in whispers and murmurs. Some were crying softly.

This was where Ben and Nya had ended up last night after their endless trudge through the ruins — to this school on a hill. They'd walked for hours. Ben hoped that one day he'd forget the terrible things he'd seen as he walked: the arm sticking out from under a pile of wreckage, the old man carrying a lifeless-looking woman on his back. He passed a young man sitting motionless in front of a ruined house. Ben went up to him, to see if he needed help. But the man just stared straight ahead, barely blinking, like a statue. Ben waited, kneeling in front of him, but the man refused to speak, or even to look at Ben.

And so Ben walked on, until he finally reached the end of the wave's path of destruction. He saw the school up on the hill, but getting there was the hardest part of the journey. By then, he was so freezing cold that he was completely numb. His feet were bricks of ice. In Health class last year, he'd learned about what happens to a person when their body gets too cold. Their muscles stop working right. Their mind gets all confused. Their heart slows down so there's not enough blood flowing.

That's what must have happened to Ben. By the time he made it to the lobby of the school, he could no longer walk. He'd staggered in, a frozen ghost with a shivering cat around his neck.

He collapsed onto the floor.

After that, Ben's memories were blurry.

There were strong arms that picked him up, soft voices speaking to him, a warm blanket wrapped tight around him. Gentle hands cleaned the mud from his face. Someone put a cup of water to his mouth and Ben drank. He drifted in and out of a kind of shadowy sleep.

The next thing he knew he was here, on the floor of the gym. His muddy clothes were gone, and he was wearing a worn sweatshirt and a pair of sweatpants. Nya had been cleaned off, too, the oil wiped from her fur. There was a bandage on Ben's hand, and more on the cuts and gashes that covered his legs.

People had taken care of him, but he had no idea who.

Without any power, the school was very cold. He shivered under his blankets, glad for the extra bit of heat from Nya's skinny body curled up on his stomach.

Lying next to Ben were a little girl and her mother. The mother was asleep, but the girl was awake, staring at Ben with steady, thoughtful eyes. Ben guessed she was around Harry's age. She had a Hello Kitty doll clutched in her arms. The girl sat up. She reached for a bottle of water, and slid it over to Ben.

He couldn't remember ever being this thirsty. The bitter metal taste of the wave coated his tongue like glue.

He managed to smile a little, but he shook his head, *No thank you.*

He couldn't take any water from the little girl.

She woke up her mother, and spoke to her in a high whisper.

The woman sat up. Even in the dim light, Ben could see the sadness and worry on her face. Ben wondered where the girl's father was.

The woman gave Ben a kind smile.

She even spoke a bit of English.

"Please," she said. "Take. You need."

She pushed the bottle of water to Ben. Then she reached into her bag and took out a bag of chips.

"Please," she said again.

He still had the feeling he should say no, that the woman hardly had enough for herself and her daughter. But he couldn't resist.

At least he knew the Japanese word for thank you.

"Arigato," he said. *"Arigato."*

Ben drank half the water and shared some with Nya. He made himself save some for later.

Then he closed his eyes and drifted back to sleep, into his dreams.

He dreamed of Dad, and this time they were together in Shogahama, walking through the pine forest, running along the beach. And somewhere in the dream, a man's voice called out to Ben.

But it wasn't Dad's voice, or Ojisan's.

Ben opened his eyes.

There was a man kneeling next to him.

"Hello, old friend," he said. "I was hoping we'd see each other again."

It was Dr. Sato.

CHAPTER 12

They sat together in an empty classroom. Dr. Sato had given Ben an apple and a cup of water. Ben devoured them both.

He told Dr. Sato the story about what had happened in the tsunami, how Mom and Harry and Ojisan had been swept away from him.

"They're gone," Ben said.

"No, they are not gone," Dr. Sato said, reaching over and grabbing Ben's hand. "People are scattered everywhere. Have patience. You are safe here. And we will wait."

Dr. Sato had a look in his eye. And for a flickering second, it reminded Ben of the way Dad would look, when Ben would glimpse him in the stands during a basketball game. It didn't matter if the team was winning or losing, or if Ben was on fire or all thumbs. Dad always looked so *sure*. And that look never wavered.

Dr. Sato told Ben his own story — how he'd just gotten to his house when the quake happened. His house was high in the hills, above the school. He'd stood on his porch as the wave hit.

"I watched the waves destroy Shogahama," he said, his face darkening.

It was no use trying to get to the hospital, and so he came to the school.

"I knew people would need help," he said.

People like Ben.

It had been Dr. Sato who lifted him up when he collapsed in the school hallway. Two teachers had helped the doctor clean Ben's cuts and bruises, find him clothes, and carry him to the gym to sleep.

"I hated to leave you," he said. "But some of us went out into the night, to see if we could find survivors."

Dr. Sato looked away for a moment, and Ben could tell that there hadn't been any survivors to find.

Before Ben could think too hard about this, two women came in to speak to Dr. Sato.

They were both sensei — teachers at the school.

The teachers and Dr. Sato spoke, and in the swirl of Japanese words, Ben heard his name. When they finished talking, the women smiled at Ben and left.

"We have lots of work to do," Dr. Sato said. "It could be days before help gets to us. The village is completely cut off. And so it's up to us to figure out how to find food and water. We have ten children whose parents have not arrived. We have to look out for them."

It took Ben a few seconds to realize that the "we" and "us" meant Ben, too.

Dr. Sato explained that the two teachers he'd just met had been here through the night. "They need to go check on their families," he said.

Ben nodded.

"And so I've told them that you will watch over some of the younger children while they are gone."

Ben stared at Dr. Sato.

He was asking Ben to take care of children?

How could Ben take care of anyone right now? How could he do anything when he was so worried about Mom and Harry and Ojisan?

But before he could speak, one of the teachers was back. She had three little kids with her. They looked to be maybe five or six years old. All boys.

The teacher introduced them to Ben: Kazu, Hidecki, and Akira.

The boys looked shy and scared. But then Nya stepped forward.

"Eee, eee," she said.

The boys giggled.

Dr. Sato said a few words to the boys in Japanese.

"I've said that you are their sensei," he told Ben. "I've told them that you are in charge."

He patted Ben on the back.

"I'm heading out with some others to see if we can find some supplies," Dr. Sato added. "I'll be back this afternoon."

And in a flash, he and the teacher were gone.

The boys looked at Ben expectantly. He opened his mouth to say something, but remembered they didn't speak English. He wondered what he could do to keep them busy. There was no power, no TV, no video games.

Ben looked out the window at the playground.

And then he saw the hoop, behind the slide.

He'd seen a net bag of basketballs in the corner of the gym.

He led the boys outside, and they all shivered in the cold.

But soon they were running around. Ben's aching muscles loosened up. The sun got brighter in the sky, and they had stripped off their coats. The boys worked hard. Soon the air was filled with the sound of bouncing balls and laughing boys.

After lunch, the boys took a break to climb on the jungle gym. Ben decided to practice his own shots. He worked through his free throws and threes. He was surprised by how good it felt, how much he'd missed playing.

At one point he stood at the back of the blacktop, as far away from the hoop as he could get. He and Dad used to have contests, to see who could shoot from farthest away. The boys stopped their climbing and watched Ben.

Bounce.

Bounce.

Bounce.

Ben shot the ball.

And as it sailed through the air, someone screamed out his name.

"Ben!"

"Ben!"

He turned, and there was Harry, running at him at full speed, his arms and legs pumping, tears streaming down his smiling face.

Behind him were Ojisan and Mom.

Swish.

CHAPTER 13

MARCH 25, 2011
NARITA INTERNATIONAL AIRPORT
TOKYO, JAPAN

Ben sat between Mom and Harry on the airplane.
Soon they would take off.

It was two weeks after the wave, and they were
heading home.

The stewardess came by for the third time and asked Mom to please turn off her phone. Mom was talking to Dr. Sato. They'd been working together nonstop these past two weeks, trying to get supplies to Shogahama. Mom's friends in the air force were helping.

Finally, Mom said good-bye to Dr. Sato and turned off her phone. She smiled at Ben, put her head back, and closed her eyes.

None of them had slept much lately.

Harry had Nya's cage on his lap. He was giving the old cat one last scratch on the head before he'd have to put her under the seat.

Ojisan had asked them to take Nya home with them, to keep an eye on her. Of course they were happy about that.

Ben looked at the scar on Harry's arm.

"Your scar is cooler than Darth Vader's," Ben said.

"Way cooler," Harry said with a grin.

It amazed Ben that Harry had come through the disaster with no other injuries. By some miracle, Mom and Harry and Ojisan had managed to stay together after they fell out of the car. The water had swept them into the parking garage of Shogahama's only apartment building. They'd rushed up the stairway, just steps ahead of the wave. They'd made it to the roof, waiting there with dozens of other people until the water subsided.

Like all of them, Harry had seen some terrible things. He was having nightmares almost every night. Loud noises made him jump.

Ben, too.

Ben knew how lucky they were to be together, that they were safe.

But it was hard to feel happy when there was so much sadness all around. The quake had been the strongest ever to hit Japan, the fourth-strongest ever recorded in the world. The tsunami had destroyed towns and cities up and down the Japanese coast for hundreds of miles. Thousands and thousands of people had died, and thousands more were still missing. There had been some happy moments at the school, like when Akira's parents finally came, and then Hidecki's. But many people couldn't find their relatives. In the end, it was Kazu's aunt from Tokyo who came to pick him up.

And just when it seemed the news couldn't get scarier, there was another disaster. The quake and wave had damaged a nuclear power station in a place called Fukushima, about forty miles up the coast from Shogahama. Radioactive particles were leaking out of the power plant. Even small amounts of radiation can make people very sick, especially children. People living close to the plant had to flee their homes. For a while, people worried that the radioactive cloud could spread to Shogahama — or beyond.

These past few days, the news from Fukushima had been a little bit better — the winds had shifted, blowing the poisonous clouds out to sea. And life in Shogahama had improved, too. Some of the roads to the village were finally clear, so food and water were coming into the town. Ben was keeping a close eye on Harry. And of course, they had their Jedi cat to protect them.

What worried them all was what would happen to Ojisan.

His house was gone.

Many of his friends were gone, too.

They'd begged him to come back to California with them.

"At least for a few months," Mom had said.

But Ojisan refused, and Ben came to understand why.

Two days ago, he and Ojisan finally took a walk together. They'd made their way into the hills above the school. They looked over at the village below. Ben could see the tears in Ojisan's eyes as he stared at the sea of mud and wreckage. But he also heard the determination in his uncle's voice.

"We will clean up," he'd said. "We will build new houses."

Already there was talk about building on higher ground.

Ojisan had turned to Ben. "The people here will rebuild Shogahama," he said. "We will work together. And we will go on."

We will go on.

Ojisan promised he'd come to visit this summer. Dr. Sato was coming, too. He had a medical conference in California, and was staying an extra week to visit with them.

The plane backed away from the gate and taxied over to the runway. Ben used to love flying with Dad, how he'd explain every detail of the plane, the meaning of every rattle and hum. Ben could hear Dad's voice now, as though he was right there with him.

And suddenly it hit him, a crazy idea: that Harry's wish had come true.

Maybe that cherry tree at Ojisan's had been magical after all.

Because, in a way, Dad *had* come back to Ben.

It was Dad who got Ben through his moments of panic in the quake, who helped him escape from that drowning car. It was Dad's wisdom that echoed through Ben's mind in those dark moments when he was alone in the ruins.

Dad was in Ben's mind, in his heart.

He always would be.

The plane started to move forward, faster, faster, faster.

Harry grabbed one of Ben's hands. Mom took the other.

Ben held on tight.

And together they began their journey home.

A TRIPLE DISASTER

Japanese is a difficult language to learn, and there are many words and terms that don't translate easily into English. One of those words is *gaman*, which means to be strong and patient even when something terrible is happening.

The Japanese pride themselves on their *gaman* spirit, which has enabled the country to rebuild after terrible events — from the earthquake and fires that destroyed Tokyo in 1923, to World

War II, which devastated the country in the 1940s. And it is this same kind of strength and determination that is helping millions of Japanese to recover from the horrifying events of March 11, 2011.

The series of disasters that began that day is known as the Tohoku earthquake and tsunami. The disaster was, in fact, three separate events. Each was destructive and terrifying and could have filled an entire I Survived book.

First there was a powerful earthquake, which hit at 2:46 P.M. under the floor of the Pacific Ocean, about eighty miles from a stretch of Japan's northeastern coast called Tohoku. Most earthquakes last a few seconds. The San Francisco earthquake of 1906 lasted for thirty seconds. The Tohoku earthquake lasted, in some areas, for more than five minutes.

Five minutes!

To get a sense of what this was like, you can do what I did one morning: set a timer and just sit in a chair for five minutes. And then try to imagine, as you're sitting there, that your whole house is shaking, that the air is filled with an explosive roar, and that you are in a state of absolute terror.

It must have been an incredible relief when the shaking finally stopped. Except that the worst was yet to come — a massive tsunami, triggered by the quake.

People in coastal Japan know that tsunamis — a series of massive, powerful ocean waves — often follow earthquakes. If you walk in the hills above Japan's coast, you can find "tsunami markers," slabs of stone built to show where past tsunamis reached. These markers were created by survivors of these tsunamis, and were meant to warn future generations of the dangers of living too close to the ocean in a region prone to these disastrous waves. The markers are engraved with messages: "Don't build below this spot," one says. "Tsunami reached here," says another. Some of these stone markers are more than five hundred years old.

But few communities have obeyed these ancient warnings. Coastlines in Japan, like those here in the United States, are crowded with homes and shops and factories. Like Americans, most Japanese people have confidence that modern science and technology will protect against nature's power. Indeed, Japan has the best tsunami warning system in the world, and in many coastal areas, massive seawalls have been built to guard against tsunamis. Within minutes of the March 11 earthquake, alerts were broadcast all along the coast. Sirens blared. Cell phones chirped. TV stations warned people to head to higher ground.

But the seawalls and warnings were no match for nature's power. In some areas, the waves were more than one hundred feet high. Seawalls crumbled like sand castles. Boats were flung to the rooftops of buildings. Many people tried to escape to higher ground — but the wave followed them. Some of the towns that were destroyed were five miles from the sea, areas nobody believed were within reach of a tsunami.

Thousands and thousands of people were killed on March 11, 2011. Thousands more were injured and thousands are still missing. Hundreds of thousands of homes were damaged or washed away. Entire towns were obliterated.

And yet, when the waters finally retreated, another disaster was unfolding at a nuclear power station called Fukushima Daiichi. The earthquake and wave had damaged the power station. Soon, toxic smoke and steam were leaking into the air. The clouds contained tiny particles that were radioactive — and extremely dangerous to humans and animals. Breathing in a small amount of these particles can make a person very sick.

Two hundred thousand people, who had managed to survive the terror of the quake and the tsunami, had to flee the toxic cloud that spread for miles around the power station. Two years later, most people have not returned. Several towns were so badly contaminated with radiation that they had to be completely abandoned, becoming ghost towns, their streets lined with empty houses, shops, and schools. Decades will pass before the towns will be safe enough for humans to live there again.

Each I Survived book requires months and months of research and writing. Most of the time, when I'm finished, I can almost imagine what it was like for the people living through the events I'm writing about. I could feel the terror of seeing a shark swimming toward me in a creek. I could practically smell the cannon smoke wafting across a Civil War battlefield. I could hear the screaming winds of a hurricane in my mind.

But the Tohoku disaster was so enormous, I really can't begin to imagine what it was like — the terror, the destruction, the exhaustion, the despair.

What I do feel — deep in my heart — is admiration for the millions of people of the Tohoku region and throughout eastern Japan who are rebuilding their towns and their lives, who are determined to move forward, and for the *gaman* spirit that guides them.   .

FACTS ABOUT THE 2011 TOHOKU EARTHQUAKE AND TSUNAMI

The Earthquake

The earthquake had a magnitude of 9.03. It was the strongest ever known to have hit Japan. It was the fourth-largest earthquake ever recorded in history. It struck eighty miles off the northeastern coast of Japan, under the Pacific Ocean. For several days, strong aftershocks rocked the region, causing further damage and fear.

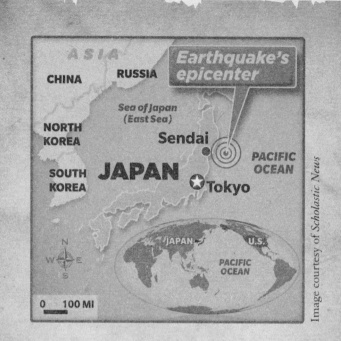

ASIA

CHINA RUSSIA

Earthquake's epicenter

Sea of Japan (East Sea)

NORTH KOREA

Sendai

SOUTH KOREA

JAPAN

PACIFIC OCEAN

Tokyo

JAPAN — U.S.

PACIFIC OCEAN

N W E S

0   100 MI

Image courtesy of Scholastic News

The Tsunami

The word "tsunami" is a Japanese word that literally means "harbor wave." A tsunami is not one wave, but a series of waves. The first in the series is often not the biggest. Most tsunamis are caused by earthquakes that occur under the ocean floor. They can also be caused by landslides, volcanic eruptions, or meteor crashes. A tsunami is different from regular ocean waves, which are caused by wind moving over the ocean's surface.

The Tohoku tsunami was hundreds of miles long, and destroyed towns, villages, and cities along more than three hundred miles of Japan's northeastern coast. The Tohoku tsunami was one of the largest ever recorded. On some parts of the Japanese coast, waves were more than one hundred feet tall. The water traveled as far as five miles inland.

HOW A TSUNAMI FORMS

1 An underwater earthquake occurs; the seafloor snaps up, lifting a column of water above it. Gravity pulls the water back down, fanning waves outward.

2 Individual waves in a tsunami are spread out: The distance between two wave peaks, called the wavelength, can be hundreds of kilometers long. Each wave's amplitude, or height, is rarely more than 0.9 meters (3 feet) at first.

3 As waves meet the continental slope and shallower water, wavelength decreases and wave amplitude rises.

Image courtesy of *Scholastic News*

The Accident at the Fukushima Nuclear Power Plant

To help you understand what happened in the Fukushima Daiichi plant — and why it was so dangerous — I first need to tell you a bit about electricity.

The electricity you use in your house and at school — for lights and computers and watching TV — is created at huge power plants. There are about 6,600 of these plants in the United States. Different power plants create, or *generate*, electricity in different ways.

Most power plants in the United States and around the world are fueled by coal. Others are fueled by gas, sun (solar power), water (hydro power), or wind. But thousands of power plants — including the one at Fukushima Daiichi — use nuclear power.

My friend Sally is a scientist, and she's willing to sit down with you and explain everything about nuclear power. But that would take a few hours. So here's the really, really short version: At nuclear power plants, a chemical reaction creates extreme heat. The heat is used to boil water. The water creates steam, which is used to generate electricity.

Usually, nuclear power works well. In fact it's "clean" energy, which means that it doesn't pollute the air. But if a nuclear plant is damaged, things can go very wrong, very quickly.

That's what happened at Fukushima. The quake and wave damaged the power plant and knocked out electricity. Fires broke out. Steam, smoke, and water escaped from the plant. The clouds and water that escaped were filled with tiny particles that contain radioactive energy, which can be very dangerous to humans. These particles don't just go away. There is no way to clean them up. They stay dangerous — some for decades or even centuries.

Statistics of the Tohoku Disaster

- Nearly 16,000 people died
- More than 6,100 people were injured
- 2,668 people are still missing
- Nearly 130,000 buildings were destroyed
  (roughly 1 million more were badly damaged)

FOR FURTHER READING
AND RESEARCH:

The Big Wave, by Pearl S. Buck

A novel about a tsunami that hit a fishing village in Japan centuries ago.

National Geographic Witness to Disaster: Tsunamis, by Judy and Dennis Fradin

Tells the story of the 2004 Indian Ocean tsunami, with lots of great information about how these giant waves are formed and their impact.

Sources

Many readers have asked me what sources I use in researching my I Survived books. A complete list of the books, websites, and other sources that I used to create *I Survived the Japanese Tsunami, 2011* can be found on my website, www.laurentarshis.com.

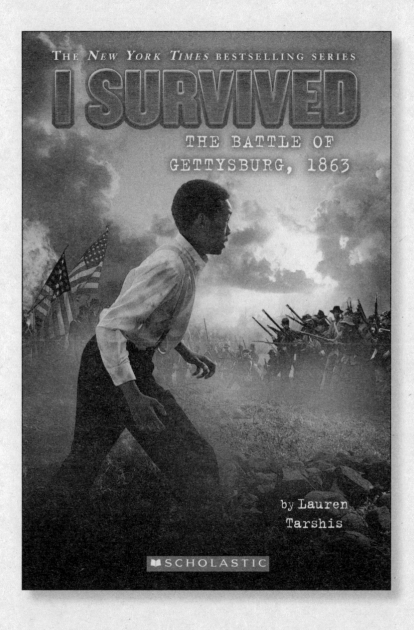

I SURVIVED

THE BATTLE OF GETTYSBURG, 1863

by Lauren Tarshis

illustrated by Scott Dawson

Scholastic Inc.

CHAPTER 1

JULY 2, 1863
A BATTLEFIELD IN GETTYSBURG,
PENNSYLVANIA

It was the battle of Gettysburg, the biggest and bloodiest of the Civil War.

Mighty armies from the United States' North and South were fighting to the death. Cannons shook the ground and set the sky on fire. Bullets flew through the air like deadly raindrops.

And in the middle of it all stood an eleven-year-old boy named Thomas.

Just three weeks before, Thomas had been a slave living on a farm in Virginia. And now he was on this battlefield in Pennsylvania, trying to help the Northern soldiers, who were fighting so he could be free.

Thomas had come to bring the men more ammunition for their rifles. He had to get away from here. He needed to get back to his little sister, who was waiting where it was safe.

But then a huge cannonball came sailing through the air. It crashed into an ammunition wagon.

Kaboom!

Flames shot up. Tree branches turned into torches. Razor-sharp strips of metal and nails flew through the air, stabbing Thomas in the leg and cutting his forehead. He dove for cover, rolling down a slippery hill. Gun smoke filled the air, choking him, blinding him. He had to get away!

He staggered across a field, coughing and

gagging. Blood spilled into his eyes from the gash on his forehead and gushed from the cut on his leg.

And through the blood and smoke was a terrifying sight: hundreds of rebel soldiers charging across the meadow, their rifles pointed right at him.

Boom!

Boom!

Boom!

Thomas ran, but not fast enough.

He turned and saw a rebel soldier running straight for him. The soldier's eyes were red with fury. His face was twisted into a crazed grin.

He aimed his rifle at Thomas.

No! Thomas couldn't die here!

Boom!

Thomas's chest seemed to shatter like glass.

He jerked back, and fell onto the blood-soaked grass.

CHAPTER 2

THREE WEEKS EARLIER
LATE AFTERNOON
KNOX'S FARM, OAK RIDGE, VIRGINIA

Thomas crept slowly toward the squirrel. It was fat and would make a fine supper. Just thinking about it made his stomach rumble. Times were tough on the farm. His owner, Mr. Knox, could barely feed his horses — or his slaves.

Thomas was just about to snare the squirrel when his little sister's voice sang out.

"Thomas!"

The squirrel darted away.

Thomas turned toward Birdie, fuming. She was only five years old, but she knew better than to yell when he was trying to hunt!

But then there she was, with her crooked grin and twiggy legs, rushing toward him. His heart turned to mush.

"Look what I caught!" she said proudly, holding out her cupped hands.

Inside was a little green snake, covered with mud.

"Isn't it beautiful?" she said.

Thomas had to smile.

That was Birdie: Give her a grimy little snake, and she'd see a butterfly.

Birdie held up her hands and looked at the baby snake, putting her face so close Thomas thought she might kiss it.

"All right," she said to the snake. "I'm going to let you go now."

She crouched down and released it onto the dirt.

They watched as the creature streaked away, disappearing into the shadows of the forest.

Thomas wondered: Would he and Birdie ever be as free as that snake?

They'd been born slaves on this farm. Their mama had died here when Birdie was a baby. And two summers ago their cousin Clem had been sold away to a plantation down in Mississippi, where slaves were worked half to death.

Clem was only seventeen at the time, but he'd been almost like a father to them after Mama died. He'd watched over them, cared for them, protected them.

And he'd taught Thomas about freedom.

He said that not far from here, in the states up north, slavery was illegal. People there believed it was evil. Clem told stories about slaves who'd run away from their owners. They'd followed the North Star, the brightest star in the sky. They'd traveled for days and days and made it to freedom. They were brave enough to run through dark forests and snake-filled swamps. They were clever enough to outsmart the slave catchers, who tracked them with ferocious dogs that could smell them from miles away.

"But then they make it to freedom, just like we will one day," Clem would say, his eyes flashing like tiny torches. "One day we will *run*."

He'd close his eyes.

"Picture it, Thomas," he'd say. "Picture it in your mind. Can't you see us? Can't you see us all together?"

And Thomas *could* see it, bright pictures that filled his mind and gave him a flickering feeling of hope in his heart.

But then Clem was taken, and those pictures went dark.

Just thinking about Clem gave Thomas a searing pain, even worse than the lash of Mr. Knox's whip. Now the only picture in his mind was one of Clem being dragged away in chains.

"Are you sad, Thomas?" Birdie said, looking up at him.

He put his hand on her head. "How could I be sad with you here with me?" he said.

With Clem gone, it was up to Thomas to make Birdie feel safe.

"I'm just thinking about how to catch us a nice supper," he said.

He sent Birdie back to their shack to weed their garden. But just a few minutes later she was back. She was breathing hard, her eyes wide and scared.

Was she hurt?

"Those men are here," she whispered, grabbing Thomas's hand.

"What men?" Thomas said.

Hardly anyone came to the farm anymore. Mrs. Knox was dead. Mr. Knox's two sons were gone, fighting in the war.

"Those bad men," Birdie said. "The ones who took Clem."

Thomas's heart cracked open.

"I heard them talking," Birdie said, her words choked by tears. "They've come for *you*!"

Thomas heard voices from across the field; Mr. Knox calling for him.

"Boy!" Mr. Knox was yelling. "I need you now!"

Thomas stood there, frozen.

He heard Clem's voice in his mind.

Run!

Thomas grabbed Birdie.

And like that little snake, Thomas and Birdie disappeared into the shadowy forest.

CHAPTER 3

Thomas carried Birdie on his back, walking deeper and deeper into the woods.

It got dark, and he found the North Star.

The night sounds rose up — the hoots of owls and the shimmer of crickets. Animals shrieked and howled. His back ached from carrying Birdie, his muscles twisting into knots of pain.

But he didn't stop. They needed to get as far as they could from the farm.

Because soon the slave catchers would be after them.

Clem had told Thomas about those men, who chased down runaway slaves and collected rewards for returning them to their owners. Their dogs were vicious and as big as mules. Thomas could practically smell the stink of their hot breath, hear their snapping jaws, and feel their teeth ripping into his flesh.

The night got darker and darker. Danger seemed to be everywhere — looming in the trees, glowing in the eyes of the night creatures peering from bushes. Twice, Thomas stopped, too terrified to take another step.

They should go back!

He could lie to Mr. Knox, swear they'd gotten lost chasing rabbits. But he knew what happened to runaways — they'd be whipped, or worse.

Thomas kept going.

Finally the sun started to rise.

The shadows disappeared and the birds started singing.

In the distance, Thomas saw fields and farmhouses.

It was too dangerous to walk through a town during the day. They'd find a place to hide and wait until dark. Birdie was so tired. Thomas brought her down to a stream and helped her wash up. Just up the bank was a fallen tree with some soft ground on one side and a leafy bush on the other — a perfect hiding spot. He sat down and Birdie curled up next to him.

Within a minute she was fast asleep. And Thomas dozed, too.

He didn't sleep long, and he woke up thirsty.

He went down to the stream for a drink. He washed the dust from his face and soaked his battered feet. For a few seconds he let himself believe that he and Birdie were on an adventure together, that maybe Clem was even waiting for him just up the hill.

But then there were new sounds:

Running footsteps, snapping twigs, the pounding of horses' hooves.

Thomas hurried back up the bank, diving through the bushes and into the dirt next to Birdie.

"We see you there!" a man's voice bellowed.

The slave catchers!

A rifle clicked.

"Come out now," another voice snarled. "Or we'll shoot you."

CHAPTER 4

Birdie looked at Thomas, too terrified to even cry.

"They won't hurt us, Birdie," Thomas whispered, praying this was true, trying to keep his voice steady.

But his entire body was trembling.

He heard the sound of stirrups clinking, of boots on the ground.

The men were coming!

Thomas stood up and was about to shout, "Don't shoot us!"

But then he caught a glimpse of the men.

There were two, and they weren't facing Thomas and Birdie. Their rifles were aimed up into a tree. And they were wearing gray uniforms, the same as Mr. Knox's sons had worn when they went off to war.

Thomas quickly ducked back down.

Something was strange.

He turned to Birdie and put his finger on his lips. Then he peeped up again, trying to get a better look.

There were no dogs anywhere.

Was it possible . . . ?

"We see you up there!" one of the men called up into the tree. "Get down now or we'll blow you to pieces!"

They were not slave catchers. They were soldiers.

They weren't looking for Thomas and Birdie!

But who were they chasing?

Thomas studied the men. One of them was very tall, with a straggly beard. The other was skinny with a bushy brown mustache.

There was a rustling in the tree the men stood

beside. A boot appeared, and then someone dropped onto the ground.

A man. He looked to be around Clem's age.

He wasn't tall, but he looked powerful. His face was smudged with dirt, and his tangled brown hair was matted with leaves. He was wearing a uniform, too, a dark blue one. It was torn and soaked in sweat. His expression was fierce as he rose slowly to his feet.

Thomas guessed he was a Yankee — a soldier fighting for the North.

Thomas didn't know much about the war — just that the North and South were fighting against each other. He had no idea why.

Suddenly Birdie started to whimper.

Thomas ducked down, pulling her to him.

Didn't she know to stay quiet?!

And then he saw what Birdie was whimpering about: The biggest skunk he'd ever seen was only a few feet from them, nosing around in the leaves. It didn't seem to notice Thomas and Birdie . . . yet.

He held Birdie tight to his chest. He couldn't worry about the skunk now.

He craned his neck so he could keep an eye on the soldiers. He wished they'd just do their business and get out of here.

"You'll be sorry you ever came here, boy!" growled the tall Southern soldier. He took a pistol from his belt. And as quick as a snakebite, he smashed it into the blue soldier's face. There was a sickening cracking sound. The blue soldier fell to his knees, blood spurting from his nose.

"What are you doing?!" the other gray soldier yelled. "Our orders are to bring back prisoners, not beat them to death!"

"Shut up!" the tall man bellowed, his voice so vicious that the other man backed off.

Thomas's heart pounded. He hugged Birdie closer, putting his hands over her ears so she wouldn't hear the curses and cries.

The tall man stepped up and kicked the blue soldier, who doubled over, groaning in pain. Then the fallen man looked up, and somehow, his desperate eyes found Thomas, peering through the tangle of leaves.

Thomas felt a strange jolt.

That look: He'd seen it before.

It was the same look Clem had had when the men took him away.

The tall man placed the barrel of his pistol at the side of the blue soldier's head.

"You're gone, Yankee," he said, clicking back the hammer.

CHAPTER 5

Thomas's mind was swirling.

He looked at the skunk. And without really thinking, he lunged for it, grabbing it by the tail.

Hisssssssss!

It reared around, snapping its little jaws. Its sharp teeth almost clamped down on Thomas's cheek.

"Hey!" he called.

The tall man looked over at Thomas, his eyes flashing with surprise, and then fury.

And then, with all of his might, Thomas hurled the skunk toward the men.

Thud.

It landed right in front of one of the horses.

There was a split second of silence.

And then an explosion of noise — screeching horses, shouting men, the shriek of the skunk.

"Stay down!" he whispered to Birdie.

But Thomas only kneeled, watching the scene of panic.

The horses reared up, their heads twisting in fear as the air filled with the rotten smell.

The men, coughing and gagging, struggled to calm the horses. They grabbed for the reins, dodging the horses' flying hooves.

But the horses broke free and bolted into the woods at full speed.

The men shouted to each other.

"Get the horses!"

"Hurry!"

"Just leave him!"

They thundered into the woods after their animals.

Thomas sat there for a few seconds, stunned and choking in the sour cloud.

Then he came to his senses. He and Birdie had to get out of there!

Those men could be back any second!

"Come on, Birdie!" he said, ready to run.

But then voices rang out in the distance.

More soldiers!

"Corporal Green!" a voice boomed. "Green! Where are you?"

A group of five blue soldiers hurried over, led by a man with a thick silver beard. They huddled around the injured man.

"It was the rebels, Captain Campbell," the bloodied soldier — Corporal Green — rasped. "They were on horseback . . . cavalry, I think. They attacked me, sir, back near our camp, when I was getting some firewood. They chased me here. They were halfway to killing me."

"I hear reports that there could be hundreds of rebel cavalry around here," the captain said. "Let's get back to camp, before this stink kills us all!"

The men helped Corporal Green to his feet.

"Can you walk?" said the captain.

"Yes, sir . . . but wait."

The corporal turned and looked over to where Thomas and Birdie were hiding.

Thomas huddled against the fallen tree, his heart pounding.

But suddenly six sets of curious eyes were looking down at Thomas and Birdie.

Birdie smiled at them, and Thomas saw their eyes soften.

And then Corporal Green held out his hand to Thomas.

"I'm Henry," he said, shaking Thomas's hand. "Captain," Henry said, turning, "meet the boy who saved my life."

CHAPTER 6

The bugle blared reveille, and Thomas sat up with a start.

All around him he could hear the sounds of sleepy men, groaning and cussing at the bugler.

Birdie was curled up next to him. She snuffled, but didn't wake up. In her hands was a little doll

Henry had made for her, a tattered sock stuffed with straw, with two cracked buttons as eyes. From the way Birdie clutched it to her heart, you'd think it was made of gold.

Thomas peeked his head out of the tent and looked around the army camp, which stretched out across a huge field. There were hundreds of tents, crammed together in rows. A few early-rising soldiers stood groggily and shaved in front of mirrors hung from tree branches.

There were more than six hundred men here, Henry had explained, just one regiment of the huge Union army. They'd been camped here for three months, waiting for their next big battle with the rebel soldiers of the South.

At first, Thomas was sure he and Birdie wouldn't be allowed to stay here.

But the story of Thomas and the skunk had swept through the camp. Soldiers came up to Thomas, smiled at him, and patted him on the back, said that the Union army should start shooting skunks out of their cannons. And soon enough, Thomas felt almost like he and Birdie belonged there. They got their own tent. There was plenty of food, and Birdie had never been happier. She had the run of the camp and spent most of her days helping two older soldiers, Lester and Homer, with the supply wagons.

Les even made her a new dress, out of an old flour sack.

For the first time in Thomas's life, his ears didn't ring with the sound of Mr. Knox shouting, "Boy! You get here now!" He didn't drop to sleep at night aching from his head to his toes. He woke up in the morning looking forward to the day — to helping the men with their chores, listening to their stories, and watching them practice their battle formations and shooting.

And best of all, there was Henry, who'd barely let Thomas out of his sight since that day in the woods. "You know how it works," Henry had told Thomas. "You save a man's life, you're stuck with him forever."

He really did remind Thomas of Clem, the

way his voice rose up when he told stories about the children he taught in his Vermont school-house, his patient way of listening when Thomas told him about his life with Mr. Knox, the feeling Thomas got when they were together, that he and Birdie were safe.

Thomas had just climbed out of his tent when Henry appeared.

"Morning, soldier," the corporal said.

Birdie's head popped out of the tent. When she saw Henry standing there she leaped up and threw her arms around him.

"I love my doll!" she said, beaming up at him.

"No doll could ever be as pretty as you, Birdie," Henry said, kneeling down. "Les and Homer are looking for you. Can you ask them to put an extra biscuit aside for me?"

She nodded happily and scampered off toward the supply wagons, chattering hellos to every soldier she passed. Thomas noticed that even the weariest men looked up and smiled when Birdie breezed by, their faces lighting up as though Birdie herself were a bright candle.

Henry turned to Thomas, his face serious.

"We've gotten our orders," Henry said. "We're to march out today."

Thomas's heart sank.

The men were leaving? What would happen to him and Birdie?

Henry seemed to read Thomas's thoughts.

"Of course you and Birdie are coming with us," he said.

"I'm glad about that," Thomas said, relief washing over him.

"You won't be when we get out into that heat," Henry said with a little smile. "It's going to be brutal. Two days, I'd say."

"Where are we heading?" Thomas said.

"We're marching to Pennsylvania," Henry said. "The town's called Gettysburg."

Henry squinted into the distance.

"It seems like we're in for a big battle."

CHAPTER 7

The men scrambled to fold up their tents, pack up their knapsacks, and fill their canteens at the stream. Already they were grumbling about the heat. Birdie skipped around as if she was getting ready to go to a party.

Thomas helped Les ready the horses for the trip, keeping his ears pricked up as he worked. A person learned by listening; that's what Clem always said. Sure enough, Thomas had learned more in the past two weeks than he'd learned in the past two years.

The men were always talking about their families and their sweethearts, their hometowns and their plans for getting back home. And, of course, they talked about the war.

It turned out what Clem had said was right: People in the North *did* think slavery was evil. It had been illegal in the North for years. Now President Lincoln wanted to end slavery everywhere in America.

Except the people in the South didn't care what President Lincoln thought. They wanted to keep their slaves. Eleven Southern states were already trying to break away from the United States to start their own country.

A country with slavery.

Here's what Thomas had figured out: If the North won the war, the states would stay together, and slavery would be gone forever.

And if the South won?

Thomas tried not to think about that.

But listening to the men each night, it was hard not to worry. The North had more soldiers, and better weapons and uniforms. But the rebel fighters were fierce, even though some fought barefoot, with rickety guns that could barely shoot. They had a ferocious battle cry — the rebel yell — that they screamed out when they were charging. "It sounds like you're being attacked by a pack of wild beasts," Henry had told him. "The sound will chill you right to your bones."

And now Thomas could see how worried the men looked as they packed up the camp. Thomas overheard Les and Homer talking behind the supply wagons. He didn't mean to spy, but they were talking in loud voices.

"This is going to be another Fredericksburg," Lester said. "I can feel it!"

"Don't say that, Les! Don't even think it!" Homer said.

Later, Thomas asked Henry about what he'd heard.

Henry didn't answer right away.

"Fredericksburg was a big battle we fought," he said. "Back in December."

"What happened there?"

Henry looked into his knapsack, rummaging around, as though he might find the answer folded up with his blanket.

But then he dropped his pack and sat down. He patted the grass next to him, and Thomas sat, too.

Henry's face got a faraway look.

And then, in a low voice, Henry told the story of that day.

CHAPTER 8

"We were told it was to be a surprise attack," Henry began. "Tens of thousands of Union troops were to march to a town in Virginia — Fredericksburg. We would attack the rebels, take the town, and then march south to capture Richmond, Virginia's capital."

Henry explained that the Union needed a victory badly, that people up north were losing faith in their army and their generals. "It seemed like we were sure to win in Fredericksburg."

Except that the rebels knew exactly what the Union was planning. And they were ready.

Henry said that the rebels had a brilliant commander, the general Robert E. Lee. Somehow he always figured out where the Union army was going to be, and how they planned to attack. Sure enough, he had figured out the Union plan to attack Fredericksburg.

"He sent thousands of soldiers into the hills above the town," Henry said. "He also sent dozens of cannons into the hills."

Thomas knew that both sides had these mighty weapons, which were so heavy they had to be pulled by horses, and so powerful they needed at least four men to operate them. Some of the big guns shot cannonballs that were even heavier than Thomas. Others shot shells, explosives that were filled with razor-sharp metal strips, nails, and metal balls. Just one exploding shell could kill ten men in seconds.

"The rebels had the high ground," Henry explained. "Anyone trying to get near those hills was going to get mowed down. And that's exactly what happened."

Henry described how the first Union regiment attacked, how lines of soldiers went charging across a field toward the hills.

"They didn't even get close," he said.

Kaboom!

Kaboom!

Kaboom!

Rebel cannons thundered hundreds of blasts every minute.

And with every blast, Union soldiers fell.

Men who managed to survive the artillery blasts were met with a storm of bullets.

"Within minutes, there were hundreds of our men lying dead and wounded in the mud," Henry said.

But the Union generals wouldn't admit that their plan was a failure.

They sent more regiments out to attack. And every time was the same:

Kaboom!

Kaboom!

Kaboom!

More soldiers dead or wounded, their bodies bleeding and shattered.

"And then it was our turn," Henry said.

Henry's regiment lined up and started charging toward the hills.

"There was so much smoke, we could barely see," he said. "There were bodies everywhere."

Halfway through the charge, Henry's leg seemed to get stuck between two rocks.

He pulled, but it wouldn't come loose.

As the smoke cleared, he saw that it was a fallen Union soldier who had taken hold of his boot, clutching it with all of his might.

Henry thought the man wanted help.

"But he didn't," Henry said. "He knew he was dying. He was trying to stop me from running into that death trap."

Cannons exploded with their deadly fire.

Men fell like stalks of corn cut down by invisible blades.

Henry managed to crawl off the field.

Other men weren't as lucky.

"A hundred and fifty-six of our men died that day," he said. "Over two hundred more were wounded."

Four more regiments were sent in before the generals finally ordered the Union army to retreat.

In all, more than 12,000 soldiers were killed or wounded in Fredericksburg.

Henry looked at Thomas now.

"Our men are worried," he said. "This is our first fight since Fredericksburg. And we need to win it."

All around Thomas, men were lining up to march, their faces grim and scared.

Something terrible was coming.

Thomas could feel it, too.

CHAPTER 9

JULY 2, 1863
THE ROUTE TO GETTYSBURG,
PENNSYLVANIA

They marched two by two along the dusty road, camping at night, and then setting out again before dawn. The days were scorching hot, and some men had collapsed on the side of the road, their faces beet red, their wool uniforms soaked in sweat.

Birdie rode in the wagon with Les and Homer.

But Thomas marched with Henry.

Henry told stories as they walked, about his parents and the store they owned, how his town smelled like apples in the fall, about his sweetheart, Mary. He had shown Thomas and Birdie a picture of Mary, a pretty and serious-looking girl with a thick brown braid. They were both teachers at a little school in their town.

Henry had also shown them his most precious possession: a small book Mary had made for him. It had a tin cover, and was filled with paintings of their town in Vermont. In one of the pictures the trees and grass were covered with what looked like a thick white blanket.

"That's snow," Henry had explained. "It comes from the sky, like tiny icy flowers. There's nothing more beautiful than the first snow in Vermont."

Birdie had closed her eyes and smiled, as if she could see it all in her imagination.

Thomas wished he could. But it seemed his

mind had stopped making happy pictures when Clem was taken.

"I told Mary all about you," Henry said now. "In my last letter."

"You wrote about me?" Thomas said, trying not to smile.

Hearing that made him feel important.

"One day you'll be able to write your own letters," Henry said.

Thomas wondered if Henry was right. He hadn't learned how to read or write; teaching a slave to read was illegal all over the South.

"Clem knew how to read," Thomas said.

Henry always liked hearing about Clem.

"How did he manage to learn?" Henry asked.

"One winter, one of Mr. Knox's sons got sick," Thomas said. "So Mrs. Knox gave him lessons at home. Clem would sneak up to the house, and stand on a bucket outside the window so he could hear."

"That's clever!" Henry said with a laugh.

Thomas remembered how Clem would stay up late into the night. "He'd burn a candle so he could practice scratching letters into the dirt," he told Henry.

Some mornings Thomas woke up and the entire floor of their shack was covered with words, as though Clem had spelled out all of his dreams.

"But then Mr. Knox caught him. He noticed that Clem wasn't in the fields when he was supposed to be, and he found him up at the house, his ear close to the window. He saw all the words written in the dirt."

"What did he do?"

Thomas glanced at Henry.

He hadn't meant to tell this part. He tried never to think about it.

"He whipped him."

Thomas closed his eyes, trying to stop the flood of memories — the *thwack* of Mr. Knox's whip, Clem's shouts of pain, the sight of Clem's blood-soaked shirt.

"Clem couldn't walk for two weeks."

"For learning to read?" Henry said, his eyes blazing with anger and shock.

"Yes, sir," Thomas said.

They marched quietly for a moment, and then Henry turned.

He put his hand on Thomas's arm.

"There are plenty of bad people in the world," he said. "Too many to count. But there are good people, too."

"I know that," Thomas said, looking around at all of the men.

He had found that out over these past two weeks.

Henry seemed to have more to say, but two soldiers appeared on horseback with a message for Captain Campbell.

Tens of thousands of troops were already in Gettysburg. The battle had begun.

"This is it!" the captain bellowed. "To Gettysburg!"

The men raised their rifles and cheered along,

but their eyes looked uncertain. Their words seemed to disappear quickly into the air, like dust.

They'd just started marching again when Henry suddenly turned to Thomas.

"I've been thinking," he said, "that when all this is over, you and Birdie should come live in Vermont. You could go to my school. Mary is a wonderful teacher. She'll have you both reading in no time."

Him and Birdie in Vermont?

With Henry?

Going to school?

"What do you think?"

Thomas smiled, too stunned to speak at first.

And then the soldier marching in front of them fell to the ground. He landed on his back, his eyes gazing blankly up at the sky.

There was a mark on the man's forehead, like the wormhole in an apple, only bigger.

Blood poured from the hole, making a puddle around his head.

The man had been shot dead.

CHAPTER 10

Suddenly the ground was shaking, and hundreds of gray soldiers on horseback poured from the wooded hillside.

"Rebel cavalry!"

"We're under attack!"

Henry grabbed Thomas and dragged him back into the grass, throwing him onto the ground so hard that the air was knocked from his lungs.

"Line up! Line up!" Captain Campbell shouted.

Thomas had watched the men drill back at the camp.

They'd practice for hours, lining up in different battle formations, shooting at targets hundreds of yards away. During drills they sometimes smiled and joked as they marched, tossing their hats into the air and catching them with the sharp metal tips of their bayonets.

This was nothing like the drills.

The men were dead serious. Even those who had been sagging during the march were now moving with lightning speed. With swift motions, the men ripped open their ammunition cartridges with their teeth, poured gunpowder down the barrels of their rifles, then pushed the bullets in with ramrods.

"Stay down, Thomas!" Henry yelled. "Get behind me!"

"Take aim!" the captain screamed.

The soldiers all dropped to one knee, pointing their rifles at the charging cavalrymen.

"Ready! Fire!"

Boom! Boom! Boom! Boom!

Bullets from a hundred muskets tore through the air.

Five rebel soldiers fell from their horses, tumbling onto the ground, rolling down the hill.

"Reload and fire at will!" the captain shouted.

Within seconds, the men had their rifles reloaded.

Boom, boom, boom!

More soldiers fell.

Black gun smoke filled the air, mixing with the dust.

And as quickly as they had appeared, the cavalrymen were gone.

The Union soldiers stood up, catching their breath, running to help the few men who lay on the ground, wincing in pain.

And then suddenly Thomas's mind roared with panic.

Birdie!

He leaped forward, staggering through the smoke.

He managed to find the wagon that Birdie had been riding in. It was tipped over.

Sacks of flour and beans were scattered everywhere, some burst open by bullets.

Lester and Homer were both in the grass, looking dazed and bruised.

"Homer!" Thomas said. "Where's Birdie?"

"Good Lord, I thought she was with you!" Homer said, jumping up. "Lester hurt his leg. I was trying to help him. And with all the smoke . . ."

Thomas looked all around, praying he'd see Birdie running across the field, calling his name.

But she was nowhere to be seen.

Soon dozens of men were looking everywhere for her.

They searched other wagons.

They combed through the tall grass.

Finally Thomas and Henry crossed the road and walked to the edge of the woods.

Something caught Thomas's eye, something small lying on the ground.

It was Birdie's doll.

He picked it up.

It was splattered with blood.

CHAPTER 11

Captain Campbell studied the doll.

Thomas could see the dread in the eyes of the men gathered around them.

"I fear they took her, son," Captain Campbell said. "The rebel cavalry has been kidnapping escaped slaves. Free Negroes, too, all over these parts. They're rounding them up and taking them south to be sold."

Thomas's mind spun. He swayed, and Henry grabbed his elbow to steady him.

"We must do something, sir," said Henry.

Other men murmured in agreement.

"I'm sorry," the captain said. "But there's a battle just ahead. Our orders are to double step it, to get to Gettysburg tonight."

"It won't take us long to find her. . . ." said Henry.

A chorus rose up.

"I'm in!"

"Let's go!"

"Attention!" Captain Campbell shouted.

The men fell silent.

"There is a battle just ahead! We have our orders!"

"Sir," Henry said, glancing at Thomas, "what does this war mean if we turn our backs and let those men carry that little girl away? What are we fighting for, anyway?"

The men seemed to hold their breath, waiting for Captain Campbell to speak.

The captain shook his head.

And that was it for Thomas.

He took off into the woods, ignoring the voices of the men calling after him.

He smashed through bushes, following the trampled path that the horses had made through the brush.

His mind kept flashing back to Clem, to the moment when those men put the chain around his neck.

That could not happen to Birdie!

Thomas heard voices coming from deeper into the woods.

He slowed his steps, and as he came over a small hill he could see them: at least ten men. They were standing around as their horses drank from a rushing stream.

His eyes fell on a sack of flour tied to the saddle of one of the horses.

But then the package lifted its head.

Birdie!

She was looking around. She moved her legs and arms.

Thomas could see no blood on her.

He almost called out but caught himself.

He squinted.

They had tied a rope around her neck.

Anger boiled up inside him.

He wanted to charge at the men.

But he stopped himself. He stood very still.

And then his fury turned to hopelessness.

The men would shoot him before he got anywhere near Birdie.

And even if by some miracle he managed to sneak down and free her, how far could they get?

There was only one choice.

Thomas stood and walked toward the men.

"Thomas!" Birdie shouted, smiling through her tears, as though Thomas could really save her.

Somehow he managed to smile back.

Thomas put his hands up.

"You can take me, too," he said, struggling to keep his voice from breaking, to be strong for Birdie.

He felt the men's hands on him, and he had a strange wilting feeling, as if he was a plant suddenly withering away in the sun.

It was how he'd felt when he was with Mr. Knox — weak and helpless.

A tall rebel soldier strode up to him.

Recognition grabbed Thomas by the throat.

The straggly beard. The cruel glint in his eye.

It was him — the same man who'd beaten Henry, who'd put the pistol to his head, ready to pull the trigger.

He sneered at Thomas. "Well, look here," he said, grabbing Thomas roughly by the arm, squeezing so hard Thomas thought his bone would snap.

A burly man hustled up behind the tall soldier. He had a chest like a barrel and muscles that bulged through his tattered gray jacket.

"This is the one I told you about," sneered the tall man.

He put his face close to Thomas's. His teeth were stained yellow and brown. His breath stunk worse than a dog's.

"Thought you were so smart!" he growled. "I'll show you how smart you are!"

He reached around and took his pistol from his belt.

But the burly man grabbed the tall man's arm and yanked him back hard.

"Easy, soldier," he drawled.

He smiled at Thomas, nodding politely.

He didn't seem cruel. Maybe he'd let them go!

No. He took a rope from his saddlebag and tied Thomas, wrapping his wrists tightly and looping the rope around his neck.

"Don't hurt this one," he said, patting Thomas on the back, as if he was a prized horse. "A strong buck like this? He'll fetch us at least a thousand dollars at the slave auction."

CHAPTER 12

At least the men had not hurt Birdie. She'd lost one of her little front teeth when she fell from the wagon. Her mouth was still bleeding a bit. But otherwise she was all right.

And incredibly, she did not seem scared.

"Don't worry, Thomas," Birdie whispered. "Our men are coming for us."

Thomas didn't have the heart to tell her the truth: that they were on their own.

"All right!" the burly man shouted. "Let's move out of here!"

Thomas felt doomed.

He'd heard about the slave auctions, where they'd be lined up like animals. Buyers would check their teeth and their feet. There was little chance that he and Birdie would be sold to the same owner.

He looked up at the sky, wishing, praying, searching for one last flicker of hope.

And then,

Boom!

A rifle shot echoed through the forest, sending birds flapping wildly out of the trees and bushes.

A familiar voice bellowed.

"Drop your weapons!"

It was Captain Campbell.

Thomas's heart leaped as familiar faces appeared through the trees.

The captain.

Henry.

Homer.

Even Lester was there, though he was hobbling and in obvious pain.

There were at least fifty more Union soldiers with them.

"We have you surrounded," the captain said. "We will shoot every one of you if you don't put your rifles down."

Thomas couldn't imagine how they had managed to sneak into the woods. But they had, and now they had formed an armed circle around the rebels.

The cavalrymen put down their rifles. Captain Campbell stepped forward.

"We have not come here to do battle. We have not come to take prisoners. We have come for the children."

The burly man stepped forward.

"We didn't hurt them," he said. "We didn't lay a hand on them."

Captain Campbell signaled to Henry, who headed for Thomas and Birdie.

The tall man glared at him with narrow eyes.

And then, quick as a flash, he reached behind himself and grabbed something from his belt. His pistol!

He aimed it at Henry.

Boom!

The tall man jerked back, dropped his weapon, and fell to the ground, clutching his leg.

"Anyone else?" the captain shouted, lowering his smoking rifle.

The rebels stood silent, their hands in the air.

Henry grabbed the pistol from the dirt.

He rushed over to the tall man, his eyes flashing with wild fury. He aimed the gun at the man's head. He stood for a moment, his hand steady, the pistol glinting in the sun. Henry looked like a different person, his eyes filled with fury . . . and even hate.

But then he lowered his arm.

"No," he said.

He turned and hurled the pistol into the churning waters of the nearby stream, which swept it away.

Some of the men gasped; Thomas knew how prized those Confederate pistols were, and that some Union soldiers tried to capture them on the battlefields, to bring home as trophies.

But not Henry.

He strode over and cut Thomas and Birdie's ropes with his knife.

Thomas picked up Birdie and held her tight. Her whole body trembled, and she buried her face in his neck.

Henry wrapped a strong arm around Thomas's shoulder, and they walked slowly together toward the road.

Thomas braced himself for more shots.

But they made it to the road, and minutes later, the rest of the soldiers appeared.

They'd captured all of the men's horses and their rifles.

"Those rebs won't be bothering us again," Captain Campbell said.

The rest of the regiment was ahead, and now they'd have to move quickly to catch up. Thomas climbed into the supply wagon with Birdie; he was going to stick close to her from now on.

Before long, she fell asleep on Thomas's shoulder.

Henry and Captain Campbell walked alongside the wagon, their eyes scanning the woods, their rifles loaded and ready.

Thomas kept a grip on Birdie.

It was some time before he stopped shaking, before he could peel his eyes away from the hills. For a few minutes he even managed to sleep.

But soon there was thundering in the distance, and great clouds of black and white smoke billowing in the sky.

At first Thomas thought it was a rainstorm coming toward them.

But no.

"Cannons," Henry said.

It was the Battle of Gettysburg.

And they were heading right for it.

CHAPTER 13

JULY 2, 1863
8:30 P.M.
GETTYSBURG, PENNSYLVANIA

It was getting dark when they arrived. The fighting had ended for the day, and at first, the news about the day's fighting seemed grim: The Union troops had been badly outnumbered. They had lost thousands of soldiers.

But then Captain Campbell learned that somehow, the scrappy Union soldiers had managed to hold the high ground. "Our cannons are in the hills," he said. "We're dug in!"

Troops had been pouring into Gettysburg all day, and tens of thousands more would arrive overnight.

The roads around the town were so crowded that the wagon Thomas and Birdie were riding in could barely move.

They got out and walked with Henry.

Thomas had never seen so many people in one place — thousands of Union soldiers. As they made their way through the town, it seemed that every inch of grass was covered by a tent. Supply wagons lined the roads. Horses and mules were tied to every fence and tree.

Henry talked to some of the soldiers they passed, eager for news of the day's fighting. But these men were just arriving, too. Some men looked more ragged than Birdie's doll. One soldier said his regiment had been marching for more than three weeks.

Birdie stared at the crowds of men.

"They're all here to protect us?" she said, her eyes wide in amazement.

Thomas almost smiled — of course Birdie would think that this was her own personal army.

Henry picked Birdie up. "Yes, Bird," he said. "They are here for you."

Thomas could see Henry wasn't joking.

And maybe Birdie wasn't wrong.

These men *were* fighting for him and Birdie, weren't they?

Fighting so that they could be free.

Henry carried Birdie as they passed a long line of supply wagons stuck on the side of the road.

Suddenly Birdie gasped.

"Look at those men!" she cried, pointing.

Thomas turned, and he too stared at the crowd of men surrounding the front wagon.

"They look like us!" Birdie exclaimed.

The men were black.

"They're teamsters," Henry said. "They're paid by the Union army to run supplies from camp

to camp. It's tough work. Dangerous, too. We've got thousands of those men working for us. We couldn't fight this war without them."

Thomas felt a jolt of excitement.

Those men were free! They were working for the Union!

"Hello!" Birdie sang out as they passed, waving madly. "Hello!"

The men looked up in surprise, their tired and dusty faces melting into smiles at the sight of Birdie.

Thomas wished he could talk to them. Where had they come from? How had they gotten here?

But there was no time. Their regiment had been ordered to set up camp in a wooded field outside of the town and wait for their orders.

"We're in for a tough battle tomorrow," Captain Campbell said. "Get rest now, but be ready, men."

The men dropped their bedrolls and knapsacks and collapsed to the ground. They peeled off their boots and socks and washed their bloodied and blistered feet. And then most of them fell asleep, not even bothering to eat supper or spread out their blankets.

Thomas and Birdie slept, too.

But sometime later that night, the entire camp was awakened by the bugler, followed by Captain Campbell's booming voice.

"Wake up, men!" he bellowed. "The time has come!"

The men staggered to their feet and gathered around the captain.

"We will march across the ridge and take up a position in the hills," the captain announced, pointing into the darkness behind them. "By morning, the rebels will be on the attack. Our mission is to help hold the ground."

Just hours ago the men had looked so ragged and battered they could barely stand. Now they were alert, standing strong.

"The fighting will be fierce," the captain said. "The rebels will come at us hard. They will fight with all of their might to knock us from those hills, to crush us. But we will hold our ground, men! We will hold our ground!"

The soldiers listened with hard expressions.

"Yes, Captain!" a soldier yelled.

"We will hold the ground!" shouted another.

The captain looked around, his steely gaze seeming to fall on each and every man.

"This is it, men," he said, his voice rising. "Everything has led to this place, to this moment! This is our time!"

Someone shouted out a word:

"*Fredericksburg!*"

It seemed to hover there in the air.

Someone else shouted it out, and then more and more, until the shouts were a wild chanting chorus.

"*Fredericksburg!*"

"*Fredericksburg!*"

"*Fredericksburg!*"

The men pumped their fists, their eyes fiery.

And at first Thomas didn't understand.

Why would they want to remember that terrible battle, where their regiment had lost so many men? Were they thinking they would lose this battle, too?

But as the chants grew louder, Thomas could see that the men were turning that day into something new, something strong that they would take with them into battle.

Finally the captain held up his hands.

"Let's go, men!"

As the men scrambled to line up, Henry took Thomas aside.

"You and Birdie will stay here with Homer and Les," he said. "They will keep you safe. You will stay with them, no matter what."

Thomas nodded.

A man shouted to Henry, "Come on!"

Henry ignored him.

He put his hands on Thomas's shoulders. And he looked him straight in the eye.

"Remember what I told you," he said. "During the march. That I want you and Birdie to come to Vermont."

"We will go," Thomas said. "We want to go with you."

"Good," Henry said. "You will have a fine and happy life there."

"I know we will," Thomas said.

Captain Campbell was yelling now, ordering the men to start marching.

"And, Thomas, we can't know what will happen out there. So I want you to make me a promise."

He gripped Thomas tighter.

"No matter what happens to me, you will go to Vermont. You will live with my family."

What was Henry saying?

"Promise me," Henry said, his eyes fixed on Thomas's.

Thomas nodded weakly.

Henry reached into his knapsack, and pulled out the book of paintings Mary had made for him.

"Keep this for me," he said, slipping it into Thomas's shirt pocket.

Then he put his hand on Thomas's head, nodded, and quickly turned away.

A second later he was gone.

CHAPTER 14

When the fighting began, explosions of cannon fire were booming from both sides.

The explosions got louder and louder, and came so quickly that there was just one tremendous noise, as though every tree on earth was crashing to the ground at once.

The earth under their feet shook.

The noise pounded in their ears.

Birdie stayed in the wagon with Les, whose leg was in such bad shape that he could barely walk. Homer and Thomas stood on a big rock near the wagon. They could see the hills and the fields below. Right now, there was too much cannon smoke to see much.

But earlier that morning, when all was still quiet, Homer had pointed out the spot where the men from their regiment were positioned: a small hill covered with scrubby trees and big rocks. It didn't look like much, especially from far away. But it was one of the highest points in Gettysburg. "It's worth fighting for," Homer said. "And our men are tough. By God, we'll fight for it. If those rebels want it, they're going to have to try to rip it out of our hands."

He'd pointed to the meadow, just below the rocky hill.

"I'd guess that, within a few hours, there are going to be thousands of rebel troops charging across that meadow to try to take the high ground."

Thomas kept his eye on the smoky scene below. Every so often a gust of wind would clear the smoke for a few seconds, and Thomas would catch a glimpse of the field.

So far there were no soldiers charging across it. Maybe there never would be.

Suddenly a messenger on horseback came galloping up.

"The captain needs the ammunition wagon right away!"

"We were ordered to stay here," Homer said.

"They need more cartridges now!"

"All right," Homer said. "We'll get it right up there."

Les got up and tried to hop over to the ammunition wagon, his face sweaty and white with pain.

"Let me go," Thomas said.

Birdie was fast asleep. He would be back before she woke up.

Homer and Les looked nervously at each other, but then Homer gave a nod.

Thomas hopped onto the wagon, and Homer snapped the reins. The horses moved swiftly, out of the field and up a dusty road.

"Keep your head down," Homer said.

The horses faltered, struggling to get up a rocky stretch of the road.

They'd barely made it to the top of the hill when there was a whistling sound.

"Look out!" a voice screamed.

There was a deafening explosion.

Kaboom!

And a tree right behind them shattered into a million shards of wood.

The horses panicked, and Homer quickly unhitched them from the wagon.

"Come on!" he called. "Let's grab some boxes and run up there!"

But then there was more whistling. . . .

"Thomas! Run!"

Thomas sprinted away seconds before a cannonball smashed into the wagon.

Kaboooooom!

Thomas felt as though his head had been smacked into a stone wall. A shard of metal sliced his forehead. Another carved a jagged gash into his right thigh.

The wagon erupted into a fireball as he hit the ground. Flames chased after him. Men groaned and screamed.

"Thomas!" called Homer.

Thomas gasped in the smoke. Blood spilled into his eyes. He couldn't breathe. Burning wood surrounded him.

He crawled away, his leg throbbing with pain. He was desperate to escape the flames and smoke.

He rolled down the hill, down, down, down, until he reached the flat grass of the meadow.

His head pounded. He could feel the blood gushing from his leg. It was a bad cut. Very bad.

The smoke burned his eyes and his lungs. It was hard to breathe, to even think.

Down in the grass, there wasn't as much smoke. A breeze blew and for a few seconds the air cleared. Thomas could see across the field.

He froze in terror.

There they were, rebel soldiers ready to charge. There were thousands of them — men in front on horseback, waving gleaming swords. Behind them, two lines of men stretched across the entire meadow, soldiers with their rifles raised.

Suddenly there was a noise, rising above the booms, a howling scream that rushed across the meadow like a raging wind.

The rebel yell.

The men were screaming as they began their charge across the meadow.

Thomas had to get away. But where could he go?

The rebel cannons still boomed, sending their deadly balls and shells into the hills behind him. Thomas turned to climb back up to the high ground.

But now there was the thundering of thousands of pounding rebel boots.

It was too late. A rebel soldier was running toward Thomas, his eyes glowing bloodred through the smoke, his face twisted into an awful killing grin.

"No!" Thomas screamed.

He couldn't die here.

He couldn't leave Birdie!

Boom!

The bullet hit Thomas, and his chest seemed to explode.

The world around him spun. The sky fell, and the air turned bright white.

Thomas hit the ground hard, his body sinking into soft, blood-soaked grass.

CHAPTER 15

Later, there was pain.

And voices calling to him.

Was he dead?

No, he was back with Mr. Knox.

That must be why his entire body hurt. Because he was back on the farm, working dawn to dusk.

He could hear Birdie, feel her little hand gripping his.

But who was that other man calling his name?

"Thomas!"

"Thomas!"

Thomas tried to open his eyes, but there was just darkness.

He tried to speak, but his voice was like ashes.

He wanted to move, but he felt hands holding him down.

Or were they chains?

Searing pain ripped across his chest.

Mr. Knox! Please don't whip me!

He was a slave again.

Or was he dead?

Two days passed before Thomas realized that he was alive, and that he was not back at Mr. Knox's farm.

He was in a hospital tent, still in Gettysburg.

He'd been carried off the battlefield along with thousands of others. His pants had been soaked in blood. His eyes were swollen shut.

When the ambulance crew was searching the field for wounded, at first they thought Thomas was dead. But then they heard him shout.

"Birdie!"

They had put him on a stretcher carefully, wondering how on earth this boy had gotten himself onto this battlefield, assuming he was a servant to one of the officers.

Most of his blood had spilled into the grass, from the enormous gash on his leg.

The rebel's bullet had bruised his chest.

It would have killed him, ripped right through his heart.

Except it was stopped by the tin-covered book in his shirt pocket.

Mary's book of paintings.

That's what saved his life. Not a rifle or a sword.

He was saved by a book filled with pretty pictures of a world Thomas had never seen.

The doctors stitched him up and left him, caught between life and death, as battles raged all around Gettysburg. They fought for three days in all. They battled in meadows and fields, in orchards and woods, on hilltops and in valleys. Streams ran red with blood. Twenty-three thousand men were killed or wounded before the rebels finally retreated.

The Union troops held their high ground.

But Thomas knew none of this.

He didn't know that Homer was killed by a shell.

And that Captain Campbell was brought down as he tried to protect two of his men from charging rebel soldiers.

And that Henry was hit by a bullet, which shattered his leg.

Thomas learned all this days later, when his head finally cleared.

And in that first moment after he opened his eyes, he thought he was dreaming, or in Heaven.

Because there was Birdie, smiling at him through tears.

And next to her was the man who'd been calling Thomas's name:

Clem.

CHAPTER 16

NOVEMBER 8, 1863
BURLINGTON, VERMONT

Thomas sat at a desk next to Birdie, carefully writing out his letters.

All around the schoolroom, children sat quietly as their pretty teacher watched over them. Every so often she came to Thomas's desk.

"Fine work, Thomas," said Miss Ashford — Mary.

Henry's sweetheart.

Thomas nodded, hoping he didn't look too proud. It had been five months since they arrived, and his handwriting was looking better. He practiced for hours every night, sitting at Henry's old desk as Mr. and Mrs. Green sat nearby and read. Henry's parents still weren't sleeping much, and they seemed glad to have a reason to keep their candles burning into the night.

"Look at mine, Miss Ashford!" Birdie said, holding up her paper, covered with wobbly letters.

Miss Ashford smiled at Birdie, then put her finger in front of her lip with a gentle shush.

Birdie loved school more than anyone, but she kept forgetting she wasn't the only student.

At lunchtime Thomas and Birdie sat under a tree. It was getting colder, and the sky was gray. Soon winter would come. Mrs. Green had already sewn three wool dresses for Birdie, and two new pairs of trousers for Thomas.

Thomas ate his lunch and looked around the schoolyard. The air smelled like apples.

Just like Henry had said.

Thomas swallowed hard, and glanced at Birdie.

She didn't have to ask him why he was sad.

No, Henry hadn't made it.

But they had come here to Vermont, like he told them to, and his family had welcomed them, just like he promised they would. The whole town did.

Thomas had been shocked to see the stacks of letters Henry had written, pages filled with stories about Thomas and Birdie.

"What a gift to have you here with us," Mrs. Green had said when they first arrived. "A gift from Henry."

It was Clem who'd brought them here, on the train, one month after Gettysburg. During that long ride Clem had told them every detail of what had happened to him after he was taken away from Mr. Knox's. The plantation in Mississippi had been a brutal place, where slaves were worked to the bone picking cotton in the blistering sun. After a year, Clem escaped.

He'd traveled more than six hundred miles on his own, dodging snakes and bears and slave catchers. "I was coming to get you both," he said. "I wanted us to go north together."

But in North Carolina, he was caught by a band of rebel soldiers, taken just like Birdie. They got him halfway back to Mississippi when he was freed by a band of teamsters, who attacked the rebel camp at night and helped Clem and four other men escape.

Clem went to work with them, running wagon trains filled with supplies.

After Gettysburg, Clem had loved being in Vermont with Thomas, Birdie, and Mr. and Mrs. Green.

But he could only stay one week before he headed back down south. Mr. and Mrs. Green wanted him to stay longer, but Clem had a new plan: to be a soldier for the North. He had already signed up to be in one of the first black regiments of the Union army.

"I'll be back here," Clem had said as he'd hugged them all good-bye. "I promise I'll be back when it's all done."

He wrote to them almost every day now, and Thomas would sit for hours sounding out every word. He could hear Clem's voice in his mind, describing the battles, the people he met, his plans for after the war.

"We'll be together," he wrote. *"Can you picture it?"*

And Thomas could.

His mind was *filled* with bright pictures now.

At first, most of the pictures had appeared in his nightmares: the wagon in flames, the vultures that had circled above the battlefield as he lay wounded, the glowing red eyes of the rebel who shot him.

But there were happier pictures, too: the memories of Birdie and Clem standing by his bed in the hospital tent, of Mr. and Mrs. Green waiting for them at the train station.

And now, in the schoolyard, he closed his eyes, and he saw the newest pictures, the pictures of his hopes: that this terrible war would end; that Clem would be back with them soon; that they would be here, together and free.

His eyes were still closed when he felt something cold on his cheeks.

He looked up and saw white flakes drifting in the air.

"Thomas!" Birdie cried. "It's snow!"

Thomas put his arms around his little sister.

And together they watched the icy flowers fall from the sky.

A TRIP BACK IN TIME

Each I Survived book takes me on a trip back in time. Sometimes I get so deep into my research that I imagine I really am in the midst of events that happened decades or even centuries ago.

I've "traveled" to some frightening moments as the author of this series — to the decks of the *Titanic* as it was sinking, to a creek invaded by a man-eating shark, to the shores of Hawaii as bombs rained down on Pearl Harbor.

But I don't think there is a darker or more

frightening time in American history than the Civil War.

During those four long years, Americans were fighting against other Americans. Our nation came incredibly close to being torn in two. Beautiful cities of the South were burned to the ground. And thousands of soldiers died every month. Nobody knows exactly how many people died during the war, but historians estimate that it was about 750,000. That's more than the number who died in all of the other wars America has fought combined. Almost every American lost somebody in the Civil War.

And even before the war began, there was slavery. By 1860, nearly four million people were slaves. They were men like your father, women like your mom and me, kids like you. Can you imagine what it would be like to be owned by another person, to be treated like a dog or a horse, to have no say in what happened to you?

To try to understand this time in history, I read thirty-one books — histories, diaries, novels, biographies, and autobiographies. I studied maps, watched movies, stared at photographs taken 150 years ago.

I also visited Gettysburg, Pennsylvania, with my husband and our two youngest kids, Dylan and Valerie. If you go there — and I hope you can — you will think it is one of the prettiest places you've ever seen, a charming little town surrounded by green rolling hills, sweeping meadows, and quiet forests.

We toured the battlefields and visited its amazing museum. Afterward, we climbed up to Little Round Top. This is the rocky hill where some of the fiercest fighting took place.

As my own children climbed on huge boulders and my husband took pictures, I looked out on the meadow below and imagined how it must have looked in July of 1863. There were thousands and thousands of dead bodies in the grass by the last day, each one someone's son or husband or brother or best friend. If we had been alive in 1863, my two oldest sons — who

are now nineteen and twenty-two years old —
would have been soldiers in the war, and it's likely
they would have been a part of this battle with
one of the Connecticut regiments that fought
there.

As I stood there, I thought of the words of a
young Confederate soldier in one of the histories
I read. He had written a letter to his sister back
home in Alabama, sent from Gettysburg just
after the final rebel charge.

"I ask myself," he wrote, *"if many years from
now, anyone will remember what happened here, if
they will ever think of those who were lost."*

Yes, I wanted to tell him. We remember.

QUESTIONS AND ANSWERS ABOUT THE CIVIL WAR, AND MORE

The Civil War lasted for four years, 1861–1865. It is a huge and fascinating subject, and I learned so much while researching and writing this book. I wish we could spend about a month together so I could tell you everything I discovered. But I know you're very busy. So here are answers to a few questions I thought might be on your mind.

Is the story of Thomas and Birdie true?
All of the books in my I Survived series are historical fiction. That means that the facts are

all true — the dates, the settings, the names of generals and presidents. But the characters come from my imagination, inspired by details I discover from my research.

Thomas and Birdie were not real people. But everything that happened to them really did happen to other kids — they were slaves, they weren't allowed to learn to read or write, their family members were sold, they escaped and found safety with Union troops.

Thousands of slaves attempted to escape from the South. They followed the North Star. They braved terror and hunger. Most died on their journeys or were captured by slave hunters and brought back to their owners.

But some succeeded, such as Harriet Tubman, who escaped and then returned to the South over and over to lead others to freedom. Her story and those of others like her are unforgettable and far more thrilling than any stories I could ever make up..

What caused the Civil War?

This is the most complicated question of all, and people have written whole books explaining it. But here's the simplest answer: The war was about slavery.

Remember, America was supposed to be "land of the free."

Think of the words in our Declaration of Independence, "all men are created equal."

These words are at the very heart of what America was supposed to be.

And yet by 1860, four million people in the South were slaves. That makes no sense, right?

No, it doesn't. Many things in history are almost impossible to understand when we look back on them. Even smart people we admire had beliefs that we can't understand today. They did things that we now know are wrong and shameful.

Owning slaves is one of those things.

But sadly, slavery has been a fact of human life for thousands of years. In America, before the first Europeans arrived, Native American tribes kept slaves captured during wars and raids. When the European settlers arrived here, they brought slaves to do hard work.

George Washington owned slaves. So did Thomas Jefferson.

But over time, ideas about slavery changed. People came to see that it was evil and wrong. When Abraham Lincoln became president, more and more people in the North were saying that America should not have slavery anywhere. Already it was illegal in the North. They said it had to be banned in the South, too.

There were big fights about this. For many people in the South, slaves were their most valuable possessions. A strong young slave like Thomas was worth at least one thousand dollars, which is more than it cost to buy a large home. On big farms known as plantations, owners depended on hundreds of slaves to do the back-breaking work in the fields. If slavery became illegal, these plantation owners would have to pay people to do the work. The slave owners were sure they would go out of business.

People in the North and South argued about slavery for years. Finally, leaders of eleven Southern states decided that they didn't want to be a part of America anymore. In 1861, these states "seceded" and became their own country, known as the Confederate States of America. President Lincoln couldn't let that happen. He believed that keeping our country together was a cause worth fighting for.

Do you agree?

Why was the Battle of Gettysburg so important?

There were many terrible and bloody battles during the Civil War. You might have heard the names of some of them: Bull Run, Antietam, and the Battle of the Wilderness. Gettysburg was the bloodiest of all. More men were lost there than in any other battle. ("Lost" means soldiers who were killed, wounded, captured, or missing.)

But there's more to Gettysburg than death and destruction. The Battle of Gettysburg "changed the tide" of the war. That means that before Gettysburg, the war was heading one way — the South was winning. After Gettysburg, they no longer were.

In the year before Gettysburg, the Southern troops had won every major battle except for one, Antietam. Many people, including powerful people in the North, said the Union should give up. They were losing faith in President Abraham Lincoln. An election was coming up. Most people predicted that he wouldn't win.

Gettysburg changed that. The Union victory at Gettysburg gave people in the North the will to keep fighting — and the belief that they could win. President Abraham Lincoln was reelected. He vowed not to give up the fight.

For people in the South, the loss was devastating. They lost 28,000 men during those three days, more than a third of their army. The North lost 23,000, but their army was bigger, and there were more people living in the North. So there were always new soldiers to take the place of those who had died.

The war didn't end with Gettysburg — far from it. It dragged on for two more years. Thousands and thousands more soldiers died. Southern cities were burned to the ground.

But the Union did finally win. And many say that the road to victory began at Gettysburg.

And some last (very important) words
Before I say good-bye to you, I'd like to take you with me on one last trip back to the time of the Civil War. So close your eyes, and let's travel back to November 19, 1863, to Gettysburg, Pennsylvania.

It's a cold and dreary day. We've taken a train to Gettysburg because we want to attend a special ceremony in honor of a new cemetery. More than four thousand Union soldiers are buried there, all killed on the Gettysburg battlefield. We listen to a speech by a man named Edward Everett, a former president of Harvard University.

He speaks for more than two hours. And though he's a great speaker, we are probably eager to leave when he's done.

But then a second speaker gets up. He is extremely tall — a foot taller than the average man in those days. It is our president, Abraham Lincoln. The war has taken a terrible toll on him. His face is worn and tired. But his eyes are bright with intelligence, goodness, and bravery.

And he is indeed a very smart, honest, and courageous man.

He speaks for only two minutes. His message is clear: that the war is about nothing less than the very survival of America. And that to honor the men buried in this cemetery, we must not give up fighting for the cause they gave their lives for.

The speech is so short, and the words are so simple, that most people don't even clap. Few think it's a good speech.

And it wasn't a good speech. It was an incredible speech. Today, the Gettysburg Address, as it's known, is considered one of the greatest speeches in American history. Read it now. You'll probably want your mom or dad or teacher to read it with you the first time, since some of the language is old-fashioned. But after you read it a few times, you'll understand it very well, and you'll understand what the terrible Civil War meant to our country.

The Gettysburg Address

Four score and seven years ago our fathers brought forth on this continent a new nation, conceived in liberty, and dedicated to the proposition that all men are created equal.

Now we are engaged in a great civil war, testing whether that nation or any nation so conceived and so dedicated can long endure. We are met on a great battlefield of that war. We have come to dedicate a portion of that field as a final resting place for those who here gave their lives that that nation might live.

It is altogether fitting and proper that we should do this.

But, in a larger sense, we can not dedicate, we can not consecrate, we can not hallow this ground. The brave men, living and dead who struggled here, have consecrated it far above our poor power to add or detract. The world will little note, nor long remember what we say here, but it can never forget what they did here. It is for us the living rather to be dedicated here to the unfinished work which they who fought here have thus far so nobly advanced. It is rather for us to be here dedicated to the great task remaining before us — that from these honored dead we take increased devotion to that cause for which they gave the last full measure of devotion — that we here highly resolve that these dead shall not have died in vain, that this nation under God shall have a new birth of freedom, and that government of the people, by the people, for the people shall not perish from the earth.

FOR FURTHER READING

There are tens of thousands of books about the Civil War and slavery. Here are a few that I discovered in my research, and that you might like to read.

A History of US: War, Terrible War 1855–1865, Book Six, by Joy Hakim, Oxford University Press, 2007
There's no better writer of history than Joy Hakim. This is part of her ten-volume American

history series, and I swear you won't even realize you're learning. Everything you need to understand about the Civil War is here as well as an amazing story about General Lee's sword (you need to read the book to find out).

The Long Road to Gettysburg, by Jim Murphy, Sandpiper, 2000
The author uses the real words of soldiers to tell the story of Gettysburg. There are real pictures, too. You'll get a very clear sense of what it was like for the soldiers fighting.

The Boys' War: Confederate and Union Soldiers Talk About the Civil War, by Jim Murphy, Sandpiper, reissue 1993
Many boys and young men fought in the Civil War. Like *The Long Road to Gettysburg*, this book uses the story of real soldiers to show what life was really like for them.

Lincoln: A Photobiography, by
Russell Freedman, Sandpiper, 1989
A fascinating look at one of our greatest presidents.

Elijah of Buxton, by Christopher
Paul Curtis, Scholastic Inc., 2007
This is a novel, but it will give you a clear idea of
what slavery was like in the years just before the
Civil War.

*Moses: When Harriet Tubman Led Her
People to Freedom,* by Carole Boston
Weatherford, illustrated by Kadir
Nelson, Jump at the Sun/Hyperion
Books, 2006
This is a picture book, but it's my favorite about
Harriet Tubman, who escaped from slavery and
then went back to the South to lead others to
freedom.

Can you survive another thrilling story based on true events?

Read on for a preview of

THE *NEW YORK TIMES* BESTSELLING SERIES

I SURVIVED

THE ATTACK OF THE GRIZZLIES, 1967

by LAUREN TARSHIS

CHAPTER 1

TUESDAY, AUGUST 8, 1967
GRANITE PARK,
GLACIER NATIONAL PARK, MONTANA
AROUND 9:30 P.M.

Grrrrawrrrrrrrrrrrrrrr!

The enormous grizzly roared with rage. Its dripping jaws were open wide. Its dagger-claws gleamed. And Melody Vega was running for her life. Mel had no doubt that this bear wanted to kill her.

Just moments before, Mel had been sitting in the peaceful darkness, surrounded by the magical wilderness of Glacier National Park.

Owls hooted. Night bugs shimmered.

But then there were new sounds. Sounds that made Mel's blood turn to ice.

Massive paws crunching across the ground. Wet, wheezing breaths. Low, thundering growls.

Mel looked into the distance.

And there it was, the grizzly. Its silver-brown fur glittered in the moonlight.

Mel's body filled with panic. And before she could stop herself, she was running as fast as she could. Within seconds the bear was after her, its paws crashing against the ground.

Mel's heart pounded with terror as she sprinted toward a pine tree. It was small and thin. But it was her only hope for staying alive. She prayed that this grizzly didn't climb trees.

The bear was just one leap away when Mel launched herself into the tree. She gripped a low branch, kicked her legs up, and swung them around. But before she could start climbing, the bear was standing on its hind legs. It swiped at Mel with a giant paw, and the claws tore through the flesh of her leg. Somehow Mel ignored the searing pain, the dripping blood. She clutched the branches with her trembling hands, pulling herself up higher and higher, out of the bear's stabbing reach.

But the grizzly didn't give up.

It pounded the tree trunk, ripped away branches, and bellowed with fury.

Graaaaaawrrrrr!

The spindly tree shook, as though it was as terrified as Mel. And then, *crack*. The branch in Mel's hands broke off. She tipped back. Time seemed to slow as she tumbled through the air, twisting and turning, and screaming for help.

Down, down, down she fell. Mel braced herself for the crushing jaws and ripping claws.

No grizzly had ever killed a human in Glacier National Park.

Until tonight.

CHAPTER 2

TWO DAYS EARLIER
SUNDAY, AUGUST 6, 1967
LAKE MCDONALD, GLACIER NATIONAL PARK
AROUND 8:00 P.M.

"Mel! I have a question for you," said Mel's four-year-old brother, Kevin.

"Go ahead," Mel said.

They were on the beach outside their grand-father's log cabin. Kevin was perched on Mel's lap, gobbling a roasted marshmallow. Their campfire crackled. The lake looked purple in the moonlight.

"What's the most dangerous, most scariest, most fiercest animal?" Kevin asked.

"Here in Glacier?" Mel asked. She swallowed the last bit of her own roasted marshmallow.

Kevin nodded.

"A grizzly bear," she said. "But only if you surprise it."

Everyone knew that.

"What animal can beat a grizzly?" he asked.

"Hmmm," Mel said. She loved her little brother more than anything. But he could drive her crazy with his nonstop questions.

"What about a mountain lion?" Kevin asked.

"I doubt it," Mel said. She stared into the campfire.

"Wolf?"

"Probably not."

"Coyote?"

"I don't think so."

"I know!" Kevin said excitedly. "A wolverine!"

Those were ferocious animals that looked like little bears but were really a kind of weasel. Mel had no idea if wolverines picked fights with grizzlies.

Luckily, their grandfather was just walking down from the cabin. His work boots crunched on the rocky sand.

"Did somebody say wolverine?" he asked as he sat down next to them. "I once saw a wolverine steal a dead deer from three wolves. The wolverine was no bigger than a fox. But it had no fear. No fear at all."

Kevin jumped up off Mel's lap. "Can a wolverine beat a grizzly?"

"No," Pops said, shaking his head. "Grizzlies are the strongest. But I'll tell you this. Wolverines are fierce!"

"Like me!" Kevin said with a little growl. He bared his teeth and turned his sticky hands into claws. Then he fell into Pops's lap in a fit of giggles.

The sound rose up into the starry sky. And at that moment, Mel could pretend that this

was just another normal, happy vacation in Glacier.

But of course there was nothing normal about this trip. And Mel was sure she'd never feel happy again. Dad was back home in Wisconsin. He couldn't miss any more work this year.

And Mom . . .

Mom was gone. She'd died last December in a car crash.

Mel felt a stabbing pain in her chest, like her heart was cracking apart all over again. She stood up, fighting tears.

"Be right back," she told Pops and Kevin as she headed to the cabin. She didn't like anyone to see her cry.

Mel hadn't wanted to come to Glacier this year. But Pops said they had to keep up their tradition. They always came to Glacier for two weeks in the summer. Mom would want them to be here, Pops said.

Dad agreed. "You love Glacier, Mel," he reminded her. "I think it's going to make you feel better."

By *better*, Dad meant Mel would want to do something other than sitting alone in her room. That she'd want to see her friends, play softball, go bowling . . . anything.

But Mel didn't want to feel better. She didn't deserve to feel better. Since it was her fault that Mom was gone.

Mel pulled open the door to the cabin as her mind flashed back to that snowy December night.

Her friend Teresa had wanted her to sleep over. Mom said no because the roads were too icy for driving. Mel begged and pleaded. And finally, when the snow had stopped, Mom had agreed to take her.

They pulled out of the driveway. The skies had cleared, and the snow seemed to glow. Mom had started to sing. "Row, row, row your boat . . ." And Mel started singing along. It was one of their funny traditions, from when Mel was a little girl. Whenever they were alone in the car, they'd sing together. The dumber the song, the better.

They were still singing when Mom rounded a curve. The car hit a sheet of black ice. They spun around and around and around, then skidded off the road.

The driver's side of the car smashed right into a tree.

It was all over in seconds.

Mel sat down in a kitchen chair. Dad was wrong. Being in Glacier made her heart hurt even more. Because everything here reminded her of Mom. Every sparkle on Lake McDonald. Every breath of the sweet air. The song of every bird that sang from the pine trees.

This had always been Mom's favorite place — and Mel's, too. This cabin had been in their family for more than sixty years. Pops and his dad built the cabin back before Glacier was a famous national park packed with people.

Mel looked around. The cabin hadn't changed much since then. It was still just four small rooms and a porch. It had no electricity, no running water. They slept on cots, read by lantern, and collected rainwater in a big barrel. The toilet was in back, in the outhouse.

But as Mom used to say, who needed a fancy house when your backyard was one million acres of Rocky Mountain wilderness?

Look in any direction in Glacier Park, and you'd see something that made your eyes pop open wider — a turquoise lake, a waterfall tumbling down a cliff, ice-covered mountains soaring into the sky.

Mel wished she was back home in Wisconsin,

where she could close the door, turn out the lights, and try to forget.

"Mel!" Kevin bellowed. "Pops is going to tell another story! Come on!"

Mel took a deep breath and headed back outside. She didn't want to upset Kevin.

"Okay," Pops said. "I have a story about an animal way more frightening than a wolverine. To me, anyway. Because one of these nasty critters attacked me one night."

Kevin's eyes grew wide. He had climbed back up on Mel's lap.

"Tell us, Pops!"

"Oh, I don't know," Pops said, pretending to change his mind. "I don't want to scare you."

"I am brave, Pops! I am very, very brave!" Kevin exclaimed.

Mel cracked a smile and held Kevin a little tighter. What would she do without her loud, bossy pest of a brother?

"All right," Pops said. "But don't say I didn't warn you."

When disaster strikes, heroes are made.

Read the bestselling series by Lauren Tarshis!

ISURVIVED